A House in Istria

Also by Richard Swartz, available in English

ROOM SERVICE

RICHARD SWARTZ

A House in Istria

Translated from the Swedish by ANNA PATERSON

A NEW DIRECTIONS BOOK

Originally published in Sweden by Norstedts Förlag with the title *Ett hus i Istria* in 1999.

Published by arrangement with Norstedts Förlag, Sweden.

Manufactured in the United States of America.
New Directions Books are printed on acid-free paper.
First published clothbound in 2002.
Published simultaneously in Canada by Penguin Books Canada Limited.
Design by Semadar Megged.

Library of Congress Cataloging-in-Publication Data

Swartz, Richard, 1945–
    [Hus i Istrien. English]
    A house in Istria / Richard Swartz ; translated from the Swedish by
Anna Paterson.
        p. cm.
    ISBN 0-8112-1501-6 (cloth : alk. paper)
    I. Paterson, Anna. II. Title.
    PT9876.29.W37 H8713 2002
    839.73'74—dc21
                                2002001928

New Directions Books are published for James Laughlin
by New Directions Publishing Corporation
80 Eighth Avenue, New York 10011

frog nit noch mir / wer ich bin gewesn /
gedenk wer du bist / und auch wirst / werden

epitaph from Colmar, Alsace

Don't ask about me,
Who I was,
Think who you are,
And what you
Will be

A House in Istria

THE MOON, OUR FAT MOON OF Istria that drives people and cattle mad, must have been the cause of my husband leaping up from the kitchen table so roughly that the empty bottles of wine on the floor crashed over, and he shouted I must see it at once, this evening, right now, I cannot wait any longer, and before I could calm him down he was gone, out into the night, clambering up the tall wall round the garden of the house next door, the one he talks about as *our* house, even though he has never set foot in it and has no idea who owns it.

That empty house!

I don't know who owns it either of course, only that

just by being there, empty and abandoned, it has bewitched my husband, but that very night he was back half an hour later, it was almost midnight by then and he had cut the palms of both his hands badly, blood had been running from his hands over his bare forearms, doesn't matter, he shouted as I tried to soothe him and help him wash his hands under the cold-water tap, there's broken glass on the top of the wall, he shouted, every inch of the top of that wall is fucking crammed with shards of glass, but I must have it, he kept shouting, that house is like a dream; and I was thinking of how it was night-time, with the moon hanging in the sky, the fat Istrian moon that had maddened him so much that even cold water wasn't any use, his blood turned the water in the sink bright red and he just carried on shouting, no, no, no, that's the wrong color, it has to be *rosso romano*, he cried, at least that much Italian my sweetiepie knows, and I realized that he was talking about the empty house again; or rather, about the color of the paint on its walls.

This happened on Saturday, and all the following morning until noon he stayed in bed, lying on his back with eyes and mouth half-open. I thought he was asleep. It looked like another hot day. He didn't move, his arms and legs were quite still and soon the church bell would ring for Mass, but my husband stayed in bed and the whole morning passed. Only towards noon he tried to say something, but his lips were dry and almost as torn as his hands though surely he couldn't have cut his lips as well, but not before noon did he mumble something about how he had to get up, after all the sun stood high in the sky, but another half-hour went by before he actually got out of bed. There he was, standing in the bedroom wrapped in his bathrobe, saying nothing, just gazing at the mess of sheets that he always tells me must be aired and stretched before the bed can be properly remade. Every morning the window must be opened to air the sheets and blankets before the bed is made, and the bottom sheet must be stretched flat and tucked in tight, it stays clean that way, he says, the same goes for the top sheet, stale and sloppy sheets bring filth and vermin, he insists, and when the sheets and blankets have been aired and both sheets stretched and tucked in tightly, he covers the bed with the bedspread. Then it is left untouched for the rest of the day until it is time to go to bed again. To lie down on top of a bed during the day is for the lower classes according to my husband, a habit of the working class, those are his very words, if the bedspread is in place or not makes no difference, we never did that sort of thing in our family, in my home it would have been utterly unthinkable, he says, although I try to explain to him that I lie down on top of the bed because of my twisted spine; sometimes I'm in such pain I just have to rest.

But this morning my husband was so miserable and regretful that I decided to make the bed for him and while he was watching, I pulled the bottom sheet flat and tucked it in properly under the mattress, just the way he wants it. There you see, you get it right when you really try, he muttered before going to the kitchen where he got himself two cold beers from the fridge, the last piece of our Hungarian salami, a couple of slices of rye bread and the Krk cheese that my mother sent me, and all of it he wolfed while his eyes almost closed again, his drooping eyelids swollen, practically black, and afterwards he spent rather a long time on the toilet. All this took less than an hour and by one o'clock he was back in bed again, still wearing his bathrobe, but now lying on his left side, no longer on his back, and the radio had to be switched on.

Please put the radio on, he whispered.

On days like this he needs to listen to the radio. Its company helps him forget the things he has been getting up to, music is my husband's remedy for remorse, and I turned the radio on for him.

There was a piano concerto. Someone was playing at top speed, the notes were chasing each other across the keyboard.

Not so loud, he whispered.

I left him in peace and went to sit alone in the kitchen with nothing much on my mind. At about three o'clock I went to see if he was still asleep. He was lying in the bed, motionless, and I bent over him. His eyes were closed. He was breathing heavily and I caught the sour smell of beer from his mouth and all that wine he had drunk the night before, the night of the Istrian moon, glass shards and blood. My husband was sleeping and I switched off the radio. But as I turned to leave, I heard him whisper to me.

Is my house still out there?

Only towards the end of the afternoon did he finally get up and dress. He was calm and did not speak much. For the rest of the day he sat in the shade of the pergola, staring at the empty house on the other side of the wall, or at what we can see from our side at least, not more than the roof and the two shutters covering the only window on the gable that faces us, a narrow window, closed behind almost black shutters, and his hands, both wrapped in white bandages, were resting quietly in his lap. The sun was almost setting before he started moving them about cautiously, observing his bandaged hands with a look of distrust as if they did not belong to him but to some other body. I had to busy myself with the chores, doing the dishes and cleaning up, so I didn't notice him sneaking out into the kitchen and coming up close behind me, but suddenly I felt his breath on the back of my neck and then his bandaged left hand on my shoulder. I turned around.

There's something I've got to tell you, he said and my sweetiepie was as pale as anything and kept licking his lips—once again, I had to think of the moon, for heaven's sake, I thought, not again, what will he hurt himself on this time—but he just looked straight into my eyes and said I've got to have that house.

Are you feeling a bit better now, I asked.

I've got to, he said. Do you understand?

That he was speaking about the empty house and not about something even worse, at first set my mind at rest, but then I remembered all the empty bottles I had just carried out of the kitchen, too many bottles for one single evening, and I thought of our heavy Istrian wine and how I myself drink only a glass or at most two in the evening, and I recalled the wine stains on the kitchen floor and on the tablecloth as well as all the blood pouring from his lacerated hands into the sink, and realizing how recently all this had happened made me feel nervous and once more my mind filled with worry.

We don't even know who owns it, I said. Nobody ever stays there.

Ask Beppo, he said and licked his lips again. Go and ask him. Beppo knows everything that's going on in this village.

But we don't even know if it is for sale, I said.

Ask Beppo, he repeated, and by now he was hissing the words between his ulcerated lips in a way that almost frightened me, and for the very first time I regretted having bought a house here in Istria instead of buying something in Slavonia or Primorje or on one of the islands, how much better to own something on, say, Krk or Cres, before the war I could even have got myself a house on the Dalmatian coast; almost anywhere in this country I could at the time have bought a house without having to regret it afterwards, even in Zagorje, a little house in the mountains near Zagreb, anywhere would have been better than Istria. This house in Istria was a mistake from the very beginning, my little Istrian house that had been just right for me as long as I was on my own, but without

RICHARD SWARTZ

enough room for my husband, far too small a house for two people, and separated only by a garden wall from the great empty house that has enchanted him.

Promise me that you ask Beppo, he said, and before I'd decided what to answer he explained that in spite of the heat a walk would do him good, even though a long walk of course would be impossible, not in this heat, but now he felt a whole lot better and his hands no longer hurt so much, thank godness, he said, hardly anything is as painful as cuts on the palms of one's hands.

So, he said, don't worry, I'll just take a short walk down the slope and have a look at the empty house from the other side, from the olive terraces below the house, close to the bottom of the valley, and I wanted to tell him that no one cuts the grass down there any more, not even Bruno, and that in my sweetie's present condition he might well stumble and fall and hurt himself again. But in his present condition he would not have listened to me, so I said nothing and he seemed content, looking forward to his walk, and before he left he told me the grounds that the empty house stands on must once have been part of a larger estate; at one time the olive groves and vegetable plots on the sloping land below the empty house must have belonged to it, to *our* house, and it was a complete disgrace that no one in this village can be bothered growing olives any more or even collect the figs, but that doesn't really surprise him as there's nobody round here who's prepared to take responsibility for anything whatsoever, and that's why Istria has no future according to my husband, no future whatsoever, and every time he takes Istria's future away I feel that he is making me responsible for everything that happens here, not to mention everything that doesn't, and that this Istria without a future is his way of punishing me, his own wife.

Olive trees all over the place, he said crossly, but can I buy any olives anywhere? No I cannot, and as for the figs, well, why even discuss them; round here nobody except the birds takes any notice of the figs, he said.

It takes Istrian people to keep growing figs for the birds, anywhere else in the world it would be impossible, everywhere else mankind uses nature and not the other way round, he said, but Istria's got to be different, of course, and at this point my sweetiepie was getting quite worked up, here the birds have their own fig tree plantations, he scolded, and when I tried to object he explained how it was just like me to step into the breach and defend everything in Istria, not just the birds and animals, but the people too, all of them without a future according to my husband, something he had actually realized a long time ago, and also that I was one of them, no better and no worse, my own wife but still a person completely without future, he said, even though I come from the other side of the Ucka mountain, that is from Rijeka and not from Istria, but at that point he stopped talking, licked his lips and left.

It was one of the hottest days in July. I dried the last plates, changed the tablecloth and decided that it was too late to visit Beppo. It was getting on to six o'clock and

Beppo has already wrapped himself in a blanket by then and gone to sleep on the kitchen sofa until the next morning. Outside, the sun was no longer so burning hot and the air was very still. Not a single leaf moved on the trees and shrubs; from underneath the leaves looked pale and almost transparent.

One of Beppo's cats, the tabby, was stretched out on the top of the wall round the empty house, a very thin cat whenever its belly is not full of kittens, which Sergio has to kill because Beppo cannot face it. His hands shake too much just thinking about it, and so Sergio has to get rid of the kittens, smashing one little head after another against the stone steps to his house, and I too find that I don't have the stomach or the heart for watching it, but now Beppo's tabby cat was stretched out up there, as thin as anything, snoozing in the late afternoon sun on the same wall where my sweetiepie had cut his hands on the broken glass the night before. Also his white shirt had been torn, and I took it with me to the kitchen table to try to mend it or at least sew the buttons back on.

When my husband came back from his walk I saw at once that something was wrong. His eyes were brooding and flickering from side to side, something that he had seen down there in front of the house must have irritated him so much that he could no longer calmly observe one thing at a time.

Who owns that kitchen garden, he asked. Someone is growing lettuce and potatoes down there.

Kitchen garden?

Don't pretend, he said. Whose is it?

That vegetable plot is Dimitrij's, I said, though it was less than entirely true because Dimitrij owns nothing whatsoever in our village, least of all land, but he'd somehow taken over that little patch of ground at the bottom of the slope below the empty house, started digging and growing potatoes there, land that no one in the village would ever dream of claiming or bother to demand should be returned to its rightful owner just because Dimitrij was using it, something that strictly speaking wasn't his. Down there on the slope beneath the empty house Dimitrij's lettuce and potatoes were left in peace to grow as best they could, although once the snails had got a taste for the lettuce, the crop of large, mealy potatoes was all that was left for Dimitrij.

Dimitrij? Since when is he supposed to own anything at all in this village, my husband asked, and I couldn't think of any good answer.

There's something I have to talk to him about, he said, and I wanted to tell him that it would be too late now, Beppo's cat had already jumped off the wall and left, perhaps whatever it was could wait till tomorrow, but there was no way of stopping my husband; suddenly he had no time to lose, I had to come along with him to see Dimitrij, it's something important, he said, it has to do with our house, and I didn't dare argue although we are not really on social terms with Dimitrij, normally my husband doesn't even greet him, not a very good idea in a small village like ours.

You've got to be friendlier towards the people in the village, I often have to say to him, especially to the women. You should take an interest in their stories and try all the tasty tidbits they offer you, preserves or cakes or whatever it is, I say to him, but he always refuses and especially insists on having nothing to do with Dimitrij and his wife. My husband does greet the postman though, and the fishmonger as well as the priest; he passes the time of day with them, and even with the poor man who tolls the church bell, who is weak in the head and all day keeps walking back and forth between the church and the cemetery, though he has nothing to do except at mass and at funerals—even that poor man he treats with respect, but it's not enough, as I keep telling my sweet-iepie, the women in our village are as important as Father Sverko to whom he is polite only for my sake, as he lets me know. If it wasn't because you care I wouldn't take any notice of the priest either, he says, but as for that character Dimitrij, I want nothing to do with him or with his wife; except now, that very same Dimitrij he now was determined to go and visit at once.

Hurry up, he said, barely giving me enough time to hang my apron on its hook in the kitchen, come on, quick, he urged me, I've got a thing or two to tell that Dimitrij, and I went along with him, what else could I do?

Dimitrij was outside in his yard. Only a rusty chicken-wire fence separates it from the gravel path that leads to the cemetery, and Caesar was there with him, his black dog that started barking straightaway as soon as he saw us, so that Dimitrij looked up from the big black plastic bag that he was rooting around in, both his hands thrust deep inside.

Well, well, what next, Dimitrij said, wiping his hand on his trousers while Caesar was barking and pulling at his chain so that it rattled across the paved yard.

Good evening, Dimitrij, I said and my husband, who is scared of big dogs, kept close behind me.

Shut up, Dimitrij roared at Caesar, yanking so hard at its chain that the poor dog stopped barking at once and fell over on its side, whining feebly. Well now, this is really a special treat, Dimitrij said slowly and smiled, such grand visitors, but there was no warmth in his smile; it was more like someone just caught red-handed now forcing himself to smile in order to gain time, and in the meantime my husband said nothing at all, so intent was he on keeping me between himself and Caesar.

Buba, Dimitrij called out as he walked into his house ahead of us, just come and see what fine folk have come to visit, he said, we've got such grand visitors today, but all the time he kept his small piercing eyes fixed on me, never giving my husband a single glance, and the way Dimitrij was looking made it clear that he was expecting *me,* not my husband, to want something from him, and therefore needed some more time to wheedle out what it might be, why the two of us suddenly were visiting him at the same time; and Dimitrij's wife came out of the kitchen holding a large ladle pressed against her bosom while Dimitrij kept smiling all of the time, and his wife laughed, a little anxious laugh, and even my husband had to take her outstretched hand.

Such grand visitors, Dimitrij repeated, though he ought not to have said it again, not for the third time, that only showed how very unsure of himself he must have felt, wondering what I could possibly want from him, and above all worrying about my husband who normally doesn't even show his face in the village coming along too, my husband who in the usual run of things doesn't even greet him, but now had even shaken hands with his wife, which ought to have told him that it was my husband, not *me*, who hoped to get something out of this visit; and Dimitrij, still smiling, told his wife to serve us something to drink, but a pleasing smile it was not.

My sweetiepie was quick to refuse the offer of drinks, nothing at all for me, he said, but rejecting everything like that was another error, added to the mistake he'd already made by not asking Dimitrij how his mushroom cultivation was going: after all a professor in Ljubljana had given Dimitrij a certificate for the mushroom compost he kept in that black plastic bag in his yard, the idea being to sell it to mushroom farms in Germany; and on top of that my sweetiepie had failed to say something about Caesar, Dimitrij's truffle dog, bought so that Dimitrij could earn his living collecting white truffles rather than cultivating mushrooms in the cellar under his house, and so, with Caesar's help, Dimitrij would improve his standing by taking a step up from mushrooms to truffles;

and my husband had made yet another mistake by not saying anything that included Caesar by name, this expensive dog that had proved to be the wrong breed, no special breed at all and useless at finding truffles, but a dog that had stayed on at Dimitrij's place because nobody wanted to buy him or because Dimitrij was too lazy to shoot him. In the opinion of the village Dimitrij is too lazy even to make babies, but Caesar could stay on, a good-tempered dog that loved a cuddle, friendly towards everybody, but not a truffle dog, in fact a dog with no talent whatsoever as far as mushrooms were concerned, least of all underground mushrooms like truffles—Caesar was a constant reminder of the family's ruined hope for the future and it hadn't helped at all that the dog had a noble Roman name with classical ring to it, the same name as the Roman Emperor who once was murdered by his own men, and therefore Dimitrij kicked and hit his dog as often as he got the chance, using Caesar's long steel chain or whatever else happened to be handy, too lazy to kill his own dog, though even an Emperor by the same name once had been killed by his own people; my husband really ought to have at least kicked Caesar or said something critical about him.

Almost any dog can be trained to find truffles, but not Caesar, and because of this my husband should have shown his regard for Dimitrij by saying something rude about the dog or at least kicked him in passing, but no, he didn't; nothing was said, instead he'd kept hovering nervously behind my back as if Caesar had been a perfectly normal dog, worthy of respect, and this too was a serious mistake of course, especially as I had no idea what we were there for, I mean in Dimitrij's house—I didn't know what my husband wanted to say that was so important. He had told me nothing, but there he was under Dimitrij's roof refusing to have a drink with him, and this refusal was his biggest mistake that evening, bigger than all the rest of them together.

Once more my husband gestured in protest with his white hands.

I only drink with food, he said, and still smiling Dimitrij was now looking at him for the first time.

Have you burnt yourself on the stove, Dimitrij asked while looking at the bandaged hands.

Cautiously, out of the corner of my eye I was watching Dimitrij who seemed to be off guard; the slyness had suddenly disappeared from his voice and face.

Nothing serious, my husband said and cleared his throat, and maybe this was the moment when he was going to explain why we were visiting like this, quite unannounced, but then he immediately shut his mouth again, and in the meantime Dimitrij's wife had come back from the kitchen carrying a tray with a bottle of grappa and four glasses, the size of thimbles. The room was completely silent, the silence of people trying to gain time, an unpleasant silence that seemed to make us all nervous, but time was exactly what my husband did not have; feet first he had leapt into this situation without proper thought and without realizing that he wouldn't reach his goal so

.

easily, that indeed nothing could be done just there and then, no preparations had been made, and although Dimitrij now was smiling at him with a glass in his hand, this was presumably as much due to his wish to gain even more time as to the insight he'd already formed about how heedlessly my husband had rushed into this visit with a goal neither Dimitrij nor I knew anything about, and so Dimitrij carried on smiling, but a rather twisted-looking smile, as if taken aback by my husband's sense of urgency which had prevented him from finding out what he was really after, and the only thing Dimitrij and I both knew was that this way of going about things was wrong; this was not the right way, without taking the time to speak about mushrooms and Caesar and the weather and then taking a glass of something to round off the formalities, and so in order to do my best to smooth over all my husband's errors though they could not be unmade, I asked Dimitrij whose portrait was hanging on the wall behind him: the painting showed a man wearing an old-fashioned pale-blue uniform, maybe an officer, and in the center of his face a large black moustache was hiding his mouth.

It's my grandfather, Dimitrij said without turning to look.

The man in the picture had a flat, pale face emerging from the collar of his uniform, a stiff tall collar with small golden stars on it, and even after having filled our glasses with grappa Dimitrij did not turn to inspect the portrait; for all of us he had poured a drink, except for my husband, who had put a bandaged hand over his glass.

My grandfather was Major Borejko, Dimitrij said. I am a Borejko. Didn't you know that?

Truly, I didn't know. In the village Dimitrij is just Dimitrij and no one here takes an interest in his full name on envelopes when bills are sent, and if there's any need at all for using a surname everybody sticks to his wife's name; her maiden name was Flego and her family comes from here, so Dimitrij is known as Mrs. Flego's Dimitrij, but for the first time he looked straight at my husband without smiling, as if there was no more need to gain time now that he had his family to back him up.

You really didn't know?

My husband only shook his head, and I saw what no one else present in the room could see, that my sweetiepie had never heard of any Major or family Borejko, and that he was utterly indifferent to the identity of Dimitrij's grandfather too; that was not why he had come.

A true Borejko, Dimitrij said.

But here in the village Dimitrij counts for nothing very much. People are saying that he is a Ruthenian or maybe Ukrainian, anyway something worse than a Pole, and whatever he is or isn't, he does not come from our parts, and now he was suddenly supposed to be a Borejko although not even I know anything about a family by that name, and as far as my sweetie was concerned, Dimitrij's family was completely uninteresting. I could read indifference in his face and I had to agree with him; just looking at that comical uniform with its little stars, the size of tin-tacks, made it quite impossible to imagine that this could be someone from a good family or even a relative of Dimitrij's, who after all has a diploma from Ljubljana and calls himself an agronomist, sometimes even a civil engineer.

A true Borejko, Dimitrij repeated. But then, what's the point when one lives in a place like Pelegrin, he added with a sigh, as if he knew what people in the village really think about him.

An excellent portrait, my husband said, totally uninterested, but obviously feeling he had to say something.

My own father emigrated when I was three years old, Dimitrij said. To America. I don't remember him. I was just a small child and he is long since dead. But as the years go by we get to look more and more like our parents, that's what families boil down to, isn't it? We don't even notice as we take on our parents' opinions and habits and even the way they look, though most of the time we've been trying hard to shake them off and lead our own lives. But even when our parents die we can't get rid of them, Dimitrij went on, and in fact the way it usually happens, it's just then that they've finally got us cornered. It's when we become older that we turn into what we were always destined to be although we didn't know it, and when I look at myself in the mirror nowadays I can see that my nose is not straight. It sits askew on my face like the nose of my father once sat.

Where would I have got it from if not from him, Dimitrij said, gently touching his nose. From whom else?

As time passed this nose that hadn't been there before started growing on my face, but it certainly is my father's nose, the one he once inherited from his father, my grandfather, Dimitrij said. It's the Borejko nose and it's been around for a long time before ending up on me, but my father had to die first so the nose could leave his face, with the result that nowadays I look exactly like my father did at the same age, my father who looked just like his father, my grandfather, that is like Major Borejko there on the wall, and all this Dimitrij had said without turning round, and I could see that my husband was about to lose his patience, both with Dimitrij and with his nose.

It's like the way I nowadays prefer grappa to wine. Later in life my father did too, Dimitrij went on, and there are times when I ask myself if it isn't life's habit to equip each and every family with only a few characteristics—one single face so that everybody has to make do with what there is. In the whole Borejko family there's truly no more than a handful of features to share, and I keep wondering if that's not the reason why what I used to think was my face is nothing but a sketch of a face or one I've borrowed from somewhere, in order to have something to hang on to until I get my real, final face from the one who's got it now, but who soon won't need it any more.

I thought you said your father was already dead, my husband said, and I could see that Dimitrij's family was really getting on his nerves, but Dimitrij neither saw nor listened to him, too deeply concerned with the Borejko family and the troubling evidence that there was only one face left for him and one which he still had to wait for, a face that would be handed on to him rather late in life.

My father had to emigrate and die before I could even begin to get a face of my own, Dimitrij said, and in the same way my father couldn't get a face of his own until it was passed on from his father, my grandfather, that is, and while Dimitrij was thinking aloud about his family's features I looked at the portrait on the wall behind him, wondering if Dimitrij perhaps was talking about the mouth under that moustache; maybe it was the mouth that had been handed down from the father and who had got it from his father, Dimitrij's grandfather, but absolutely nothing else—not the eyes nor the ears, not the way the hairline started on the forehead, not even the nose, so unlike the one Dimitrij had been fingering on his own face, not the chin, forehead nor hair; and of the mouth he might have inherited nothing was visible, hidden under a black moustache that Dimitrij did not have, blond and clean-shaven as he was.

Looking at it that way, my entire face has bit by bit been given to me by members of the Borejko family, Dimitrij said, so that each one of them would instantly be able to recognize it as his own face. This is what tradition is about, isn't it? Tradition keeps a family together, he added and sounded quite pleased, and like my father and my grandfather before him, I too have stopped drinking wine, Dimitrij declared and turned round, raising his glass of grappa to the portrait as if he had suddenly remembered that he had forgotten to drink to the deceased uniformed person, to toast him in grappa instead of wine, out of gratitude for all the gifts that had been handed down to him, and I was watching my husband, knowing that by now he was getting quite angry, that he had had enough of the Borejko family.

But just as I was planning to say something to divert us as nicely as possible from Dimitrij's relatives, Dimitrij put his glass down and asked if we would like to see a picture of his father, the Major's son, and before we had time to say anything he pulled out a drawer in the small table in front of him. I was sitting next to him on the sofa and could see that the drawer was full of photographs, all mixed up higgledy-piggledy. There, in that drawer, the Borejko family was stored, regardless of generation or rank, a family that had left nothing except for a face to Dimitrij. Now he wanted to find his father; the major's son was the only one that Dimitrij was interested in and he kept poking about, carefully pushing out of the way photos of people who were of no account now, cousins maybe, or very distant relatives who accidentally happened to have ended up on top of the rest, old and young, randomly mixed regardless of how they were related to each other: a little boy with bobbed hair riding on a rocking-horse; a stern-looking lady; a chimney-sweep with a pig in his arms; several gentlemen in funny hats and an infant lying on its tummy on a fur rug; a group of students, all with the pale smooth faces that go with consumption and other incurable diseases, all of them with canes in their hands. Still none of the photos was the right one, and Dimitrij kept searching in the drawer for his father, using both his hands very much the way he had rummaged in the black plastic bag full of mushroom compost, as if a family could be a kind of crop or a black sack we all are put into.

But he was here just the other day, Dimitrij sighed, looking for his father in the drawer, and I had to ask myself who could possibly keep track of a family like that; surely no one who had married into it and probably hard even for Dimitrij himself, and then, all of a sudden— there he was at the bottom of the Borejko family drawer. Using both hands, Dimitrij carefully lifted his father up to show him to us, a sepia-colored photo mounted on stiff cardboard.

My father, Dimitrij said.

Taborstrasse/Wien, Ateljé Löwy, was written in gilt lettering underneath the photograph, and from what we could see of the man in the photo he did not look the least bit like Dimitrij, which rather cast doubt over the strength of tradition in this family, and judging by the untidy drawer the Borejko family was not in much better shape than Dimitrij's own house, built directly on the ground, its brickwork exposed, with no wallpaper on the inside or plastering on the outside, surrounded by that paved yard fenced in with chicken wire, nothing but a house built on sand, though according to Dimitrij with the most spectacular view in all of Istria, a view that he cannot get enough of and is best to enjoy from inside the house, which is why Dimitrij spends most of his time indoors, taking no interest in what the house looks like from the outside, not hearing what is said about it among the people who pass by every Sunday, all those widows and old women on their way to the cemetery with flowers and candles.

Poor dear old Dad, Dimitrij said, addressing the photo and not us, just as he ignores the Sunday gossip on the other side of the chicken wire; it doesn't concern him, he's too engrossed in his wonderful view to care, and now he kept speaking to his dead émigré father, paying no attention to the guests in his house, and the only day of the week when Dimitrij treats his dog to anything better than kicks and beatings is on Sundays when Caesar is allowed to leap at the chicken wire and bark, frightening the people on the other side of the fence, all those widows and old ladies who after Mass pass Dimitrij's house carrying flowers and candles and wreaths, people who at least have a grave to visit, black widows and old folk on the way to their family graves, and Caesar is allowed to bark at them, throwing himself against the chicken wire.

Unlike the rest of us, Dimitrij has no family grave here. There is no headstone in the cemetery incised with the name Borejko, so that in our village the Borejko family has to be content with a single drawer, and I felt sorry for Dimitrij, though people in the village believe him to be something of a philosopher, a stranger satisfied with what nature has to offer outside his window instead of putting up wallpaper or repairing his house; and his foreign blood must be the source of his problems people say in our village, his Ruthenian or Ukrainian blood, a blood far too thin, making people feeble and dreamy, without the strength to work and keep order, the thin kind of blood this village thinks little of.

Is it not true that Dimitrij just sits there in his house, day in and day out, staring at his view? Outside the clouds are drifting past in the sky, the sun rises and sets, and what he fails to actually do in his house happens in his head instead, a long string of fantasies and dreams that need no raking and weeding and turning. No dream ever was of any use for tilling a field or mortaring a chimney, but that's Dimitrij, as everyone in the village says, our Dimitrij, in fact a poor soul like the rest of us, but not from here and only married into the village, an outsider, a Ukrainian of some sort, not even a Pole, a useless dreamer filling his belly with potatoes grown in soil that doesn't even belong to him, getting satisfaction from looking at a view that anyone could see anytime. True enough, he seems content with his view as if he didn't need anything else, not minding his scruffy house or that the white truffles stay underground, although he would have done better to dig them up instead of potatoes, but then everybody agrees that it's all due to his Ruthenian blood, so different from the rest of the blood in our village, that thick, bluish-black, slow-flowing blood like the very best olive oil, our village-blood dripping from the slit throats of chickens, spurting from stuck pigs and which some-times can rush to people's heads, from time to time rush-ing to the pretty empty-headed ones, all of which irri-tates my sweetiepie who says that there are some villagers who deserve to have their heads chopped off.

But here, in our village, they have always been proud of their blood. Only I don't want to have anything to do with it. Never have I been able to stand the sight of blood; it makes me sick, and each year at slaughtering time I keep away from the village—as if I haven't had enough of that kind of thing with my sweetie and his choleric fits of fury; his blood pressure, far too high, which he doesn't attend to; the medicine he forgets to take, and, as if that wasn't enough, his hands that he cut so badly last night, lacerated and dripping with blood before they got covered in bandages.

This was taken just before he stopped drinking wine, Dimitrij said and held the photo of his father so close to his eyes that no one else could see a thing.

My father, Dimitrij said. The Inspector General! Pro-moted by Krumholz himself.

How do you know, my husband asked and Dimitrij looked up in surprise, but didn't answer the question.

How do you know, my husband asked again.

Know what?

How do you know all these things about a father you hardly even met? Like what he used to drink or not drink?

For a long time Dimitrij stared at my husband and then he looked at his wife, as pale and lackluster as ever, even though someone was now actually looking at her. Mostly nobody notices Dimitrij's wife at all or at best someone might speak to her about the weather or the children she doesn't have, so she must have been more confused and insecure than usual but flattered too, as my husband had offered to shake hands with her, a bandaged hand, but still; this kind of attention was surely more than she could have hoped for and now she was trying to smile at her husband and my sweetie all at the same time, yes, Krumholz, she said with a nod, but her smile and what she said only seemed to heighten the general feeling of unease in the room. Dimitrij made a face and once more his wife laughed nervously, as if relieved that nothing more would be asked of her and that she would soon be forgotten again.

Of course, you're quite right, Dimitrij finally said and the smile had returned to his face again, that malicious, cunning smile for gaining time. It's true that I was just a child when my father died. But we Borejkos have a long memory, we even remember things we have not actually experienced. That's how it is in our family. It's called blood ties. Believe me, Dimitrij said, such ties can almost replace a living father. The right blood can even keep the dead alive.

You don't say, my husband said.

But not in all families, of course, Dimitrij said. In some families there're good reasons for not remembering anything at all. I'm sure you know what I mean.

What are you trying to say, my husband asked. His

face looked as if it had been drawn with wet chalk, but Dimitrij kept smiling and looking straight at him.

Don't worry, he said. I'm sure you're well brought up. Anyone can see that you've been taught good table manners, handling your knife and fork properly, that kind of thing. I bet you know complete place settings, what goes to the left of the plate and what to the right, Dimitrij said and leaned back on the sofa, still smiling at my husband.

Whatever you might have been taught by your family it doesn't seem to include keeping your mouth shut and not airing opinions about matters that are none of your business, my husband said, and at that moment I realized it was high time we went home but it was already too late, and Dimitrij was still sitting there on the sofa smiling, the malevolent smile didn't leave his face, and still he had not finished with my sweetiepie.

Nice manners are all very well, Dimitrij went on. I do try to stay polite as long as possible. But there are times when politeness gets in the way of more important things. Like frankness. That's something else my family taught me.

You're taking liberties, my husband said.

I'm a Borejko, Dimitrij said abruptly. Suddenly the smile had vanished from his face.

So that's what you are, my husband said. A Borejko? But then you might perhaps explain to me if your noble background includes the tradition of digging passages into other people's property? Or is there some rule about only tunneling into empty houses?

What house?

Our house, my sweetiepie said.

Once more Dimitrij's face emptied as if he could have been an orphan despite the family picture on the wall, and instead of inheriting his face he had picked it up from the gutter.

The smile was gone from his face. There was nothing there any longer to help him gain time and cover up his surprise, and this would have been the right moment to leave; this was the moment I should have got up and said it was time to go home, high time, late as it was, the very moment when I should have thanked Dimitrij and his wife for our chat and also for the opportunity to get acquainted with some distinguished members of the Borejko family, but I stayed on the sofa and my husband said nothing to help, only something that made things even worse, into *our* house, he said, you have dug a tunnel straight in under our house from the plot you apparently consider your kitchen garden, and of course this was the very moment when I should've stood up to say goodbye, but instead my husband got up, not to say goodbye and leave, but to emphasize what he'd just been saying.

Why don't you sit down, Dimitrij urged and turned pleadingly to me. Why doesn't he sit down? Can't you tell your husband to sit down?

What are you up to in my house, my husband asked but Dimitrij did not reply, he only put his father back among the other photographs, shut the drawer and rose from the sofa.

Buba, he asked, where are my cigarettes?

But without waiting for an answer he left the room and when he returned a little later he had a cigarette stuck between his lips, that's one of my cigarettes, his wife said, yes yes, Dimitrij muttered without taking the cigarette out of his mouth. Again he settled on the sofa and said to my husband, who was still standing behind his chair, well now, so that is *your* house, and my sweetie said yes, and you've dug a tunnel into it.

So, he owns a house here in our village, Dimitrij said, and it was hard to work out if he was addressing his wife or talking to himself, his glance was wandering round the room, somehow suggesting that whatever was going on had nothing to do with him, and there we were, thinking it was his wife who owned a house in our village, he said. Isn't that so, Buba? But we must have made some mistake as the empty house seems to be his now as if it had been waiting all those years for him or anybody else to just come along, Dimitrij said and pointed at my sweetie. Imagine! He's taken over the empty house and now he stands there accusing me of having broken into *his* house.

But I know your sort, Dimitrij said and his voice suddenly grew louder. You're a drunk and I spotted it at once.

He was staring straight at my husband who had gripped the chair in front of him with both his bandaged hands, as soon as you turned up in the village I knew you for what you are, Dimitrij said to my husband, one of those always looking for an excuse to drink. Oh yes! I know your sort and when you've had your fill and there's no room for anymore inside you, the next thing you've got to do is invent some story to explain why you're not drinking, and I found what Dimitrij was saying painful enough, but this was going much too far even though my husband had been asking for trouble; but by now there was no way of stopping Dimitrij, people like you cling to any reason to get more to drink or not to drink at all when you're too hung over to manage any more, Dimitrij said. A drunk, that's what you are, and of course I saw it straightaway, just a boozer even though you think too highly of yourself to stagger about outside and fall over, like Beppo, and my husband's face was as white as his bandaged hands.

No, that's not your style, Dimitrij went on. You are one of those who get smashed in secret, sitting alone at home with your bottle and a bread roll, trying to tell yourself you're eating but in fact it's all drinking, nothing but drinking. But make no mistake, I know your sort alright. Any reason at all and you'll have a drink or three. A house that doesn't belong to you, any old lie is as good as another, anything to hide that you care for nothing except the bottle. But now you're under my roof and here I let no drunk call me a burglar, Dimitrij said, is that clear?

What's all this bullshit, Borejko, my husband shouted and this was the first time he used the name Dimitrij had claimed for himself and put such store by, a name that meant nothing to us but now unexpectedly came in handy.

So you call it bullshit, Dimitrij said and smiled. Did you hear him, Buba? Bullshit he called it! Perhaps he's not so stupid after all, don't you think, eh, Buba, and Dimitrij kept speaking to his wife as if there was no one else in the room, you heard him, Buba, he called it bullshit, Dimitrij said in a loud voice and his wife laughed nervously.

That's enough, my husband shouted.

So you think that's enough, Dimitrij said. You've got enough now, have you? But perhaps there is something you know about the empty house that we don't? Maybe it's you who owe us an explanation?

I've seen that tunnel with my own eyes, my husband shouted, and by now I had stood up and put my hand on his arm and Dimitrij got up too, shit, he screamed, shit plain and simple, get that, nothing but shit! For two hundred years the shit from that house went down the pipe, he screamed. The drain ended on that slope, piles of common dung, that's how it was done before the better class of people, your sort, started shitting in toilets, Dimitrij screamed. Do you understand? Shit is all the owners of that house left behind, nothing but their own shit, but that's fine with me, I'm grateful for what they've done for my lettuce, Dimitrij shouted at the top of his voice, though I couldn't help thinking that he would have done better to stick to his potatoes; the snails had already finished all his lettuce, and meanwhile I was stroking my sweetie's back to calm him down, but cautiously so that his rage wouldn't suddenly turn my way, though I had to admit that what Dimitrij said rang true for such an old house that had been standing empty for a long time, the lettuce and potatoes in Dimitrij's kitchen garden seemed to prove his point.

Just where the drain surfaced would be the best place for a vegetable plot, there the soil was at its best, even though the house being empty meant that it wasn't fertilized any more, and I tried to think of something to say about Dimitrij's lettuce and potatoes as some kind of apology for all my husband's mistakes, something to show my esteem for the potatoes and maybe even the lettuce, in order to end the fight about the tunnel that was just a drain after all, but before I'd plucked up enough courage the electrical light started wavering; the lamp over the table and the bare bulb near the front door were flickering, the light was going off and on and then off again, and suddenly there was a thunderclap just above the house, it sounded as if the roof was caving in. The storm was right over us. But there the light was back again, a weak uncertain light, and outside a rumbling thunder rolled through the valley.

Goodbye to the long hot month of July, goodbye to all the still and suffocating days without air!

At last the storm was coming our way, and against the storms from the south there is no protection. The north wind in the winter is bad enough, but nothing can stop the summer wind from the south, breaking the branches off the trees, tossing them around as it tears through the gardens of Pelegrin, rushing down over hillsides and abysses, and it is the sea beyond the horizon that sends us such storms, the green sea which in the summer finds its way even up to us in the hills, that gives us weather so bad that the leaves on the trees blacken and freeze. But still more terrifying than these summers with storms are the summers when the sea doesn't reach us at all, when the sun keeps scorching the grass and the leaves and everything that grows in our gardens and in the wild land around our village, summers when cracks open in the skin of people and cattle, our Istrian summers without the sea, with constipation and permanent headache, a time when the mussels swell the way they normally never do except under a full moon or so our fishmonger says, mussels that during such summers are at their best and can cure fatigue, although my husband calls it all superstition, my sweetiepie who is a stranger here and refuses to believe in weather, having no idea of what the moon and the sea can do to us here in Istria.

But now it had arrived at last, the storm was over our heads and Dimitrij told us to hurry off home before the rain started, quick, quick and Buba opened the door into the night for us.

Once more my sweetie had to hold out his hand to her, a shiny white hand in the darkness, but he did not offer to shake hands with Dimitrij and in the yard we passed Caesar, whining and pressing himself against the wall of the house for fear of the thunder, the noblest member of this family, a useless dog, bearing the name of a murdered Emperor.

Hurry, hurry, Dimitrij called after us, and before I could open the gate to our own garden I felt the first heavy raindrops falling on my face, drops I couldn't see in the darkness—one of these invisible night rainfalls that the wind drives horizontally against garden walls and houses, turning stone and indoor plaster dark—drenching my flowerbeds, so that only stalks and broken leaves are left behind—and when I got inside I pulled the telephone jack from the wall and then hurried into the garden to take down the wash.

The wind tore at the damp sheets in the darkness, whipping them into my face, sheets that hadn't had time to dry, but still there was time to rescue them from the rain and I patted along the line in the darkness, taking down our sheets one by one, wet and stiff sheets that the wind wrapped round me, and when I got back into the kitchen I had forgotten about the shutters; they were banging back and forth, and outside the flashes of lightning were illuminating the sky and the valley below, one flash after another, bringing light into the darkness.

I closed and secured the shutters and then stopped for a moment, standing there panting in the kitchen. In the darkness all I could hear for a moment was my own breathing, but suddenly from outside there was another sound, a steadily growing, rustling noise of rushing water as if someone had opened a gigantic faucet; and this was the rain, this swelling, soothing sound in the darkness, and only there in my kitchen, for the first time that day, I felt my back aching again and hurting badly. I sat down at the kitchen table and tried to stay as still as possible, alone with my aches and pains, giving way to it all, trying not to be tense, not offering any resistance, but letting everything that was painful and hurting spread throughout my body so that it soon would be over again. My face was wet and I did not know if it was from tears or the rain or the washing, just that something wet was trickling down over my cheeks and no one was there to see it, my husband had already gone to bed.

Outside the rain was crashing down and I found the storm restful. It was so much bigger and stronger than I was, much stronger too than all that ached and hurt inside me, giving me a sense of rest and comfort that was of more use than if my sweetiepie had come out with me in the darkness to help with taking in the wash, I mean if he had done that instead of going to bed, but that was the kind of storm it was, cleansing and bringing relief.

Don't resist, I told myself, just don't struggle against what hurts and aches, and there in front of me on the kitchen table lay the sheets that I had saved, and I leaned forward over the table and gave way to my pain. When my back no longer hurt me and I had dealt with what was left to do in the kitchen, I went to the bedroom where my husband was already asleep in bed.

He slept, far from all the mistakes and disappointments of the day. The sheet covered his head but I pulled it back and looked at him. He slept with his mouth open. I sat down on the edge of the bed. Gently, so I would not wake him up, I stroked his wavy gray hair all the way down to the back of his neck with its tight curls, and I knew that now, given everything that had happened, I had no choice, because I too would go crazy if it would go on like this, so the first thing I had to do tomorrow morning, if the rain let me, was to find Beppo and talk to him.

In the morning the following day, it was a Monday, I walked across to Beppo's place with a few pieces of cake wrapped in paper in order to ask him about the empty house. The air was fresh and clear. The empty sky had been swept clean during the night, but the sun was already back in place, not even the southern storms have any power over the sun here in Istria. Like every morning Beppo was sitting under the fig tree in his yard with his legs stiffly stretched out, red in the face, but he had not started drinking yet; it was too early in the day, Bruno does not open up until eleven o'clock.

Beppo, I said, my husband wants to buy the empty house. I do not know what's got into him, but he's taken to climbing the walls at night and who knows what he might be up to there on the other side. *Caro mio Beppo*, whose house is it, I asked, whom does it belong to? Please tell me for God's sake, I myself have no idea, for as long as I can remember it's been standing there empty and locked up and no one used to climb the wall before, none of us did, to an empty house that's locked, I said to Beppo, no one from round here would do such a thing. For us it would be unthinkable, but my husband is not from here and he's at it now, back and forth he climbs over the wall, even in full moonlight and it frightens me, thinking of what he will do if he cannot buy it and won't be allowed to find what he's looking for there on the other side of the wall, and if he doesn't, nothing here will ever be the same again. Beppo, do you hear what I'm saying? You won't be left in peace any longer either.

Please, who owns that house, I asked, and Beppo looked up at me, all I could see were the broken glasses in the middle of his red face, and then he pointed towards the cemetery, straight westwards, towards Trieste, and muttered something like Signora Tina or maybe Nina, but I couldn't get another thing out of him and gave up.

Still it was too early in the day, but I gave him my nicely wrapped cakes and with the cakes I pressed some money into Beppo's hand, after all it was getting on eleven o'clock, his thirst is strongest in the morning and Bruno's inn would soon open.

When I came back, my sweetiepie stood outside our house, freshly shaven.

Fine day, my husband said yawning. He was peering at the sun and I told him that we have to drive to Buzet. You drive, was all he said, not asking what we were supposed to do in Buzet. My husband must have been in a good mood for he usually avoids Buzet; down there on the plain it is too hot for him, such a big heat in such a small town is not good for his blood pressure. But this morning he whistled the way he does only when he is really pleased with himself, he was whistling *Komm mit mir nach Varazdin*, Lehár is not his cup of tea, but Kálmán is another matter; when in a good mood he will whistle one Kálmán tune after another, but as for myself I cannot tell the difference between one and the other although my husband says that he just can' t believe it, that it's completely impossible that someone should be so lacking an ear for music as to fail to hear the difference between Lehár and Kálmán, the latter admired even by Arnold Schönberg, and to demonstrate the difference between music and what just pretends to be music as he puts it, my husband will occasionally whistle something by Lehár after a whole day of whistling Kálmán melodies, just one Lehár tune to let this be an example to me; given a little time even my wife will surely be able to learn the difference between music and what just pretends to be music, he says, and when he has finished whistling a complete Lehár melody, just to let this be a lesson to me, he turns to me and asks if I heard the difference.

Yes, I say, although I've heard no difference; it all sounds the same to me and I say "yes" only to keep him happy, and then my husband's eyes go dark on behalf of fine music, and his good mood disappears. It was Kálmán, he says. Not Lehár. I carried on whistling Kálmán just to test you.

I knew it, he would then go on, nothing I care for matters to you the least bit, but this morning he seemed content and pleased with himself. He sat beside me in the car, arms crossed over his chest, whistling maybe

Kálmán or maybe Lehár, but without demanding that I ascertain which was which, a sure sign of my sweetie's excellent temper that Monday morning. In downtown Buzet I turned right, crossed the bridge and drove uphill along the narrow street to the Land Surveyor's office, the highest point of the old city and just above the house where our priest, Father Sverko, lives, and there I parked the car in front of the gate to the Surveyor's office, a spot where the cobbles have worn smooth and soft, almost like skin. The sun was high in the sky by then and the stones had soaked up the heat already, but the office was empty, no proper staff seemed to be around. It was noon and the senior officials had already gone back home where they would stay behind closed shutters for the rest of the day. The only person there was sitting behind a desk, a woman in a blue smock and with single hairs sprouting from her face like a straggling beard.

Good Lord, what have you done to your hands, she exclaimed when she looked up from the file on her desk and caught sight of us.

Is he in pain?

But I told her that we had come to have a look at some of her archives, the Property Register if possible, and, to be more precise, the Register for Pelegrin, and my husband bowed to her and began explaining that his hands were nothing to worry about, not at all, soon the wounds would be healed. My hands have already stopped hurting, my husband said, they just ache a bit before I go to sleep, Good Lord, the woman behind the desk said, and then, ah yes, Pelegrin, now let me see, Pelegrin, isn't that on the way to Motovun?

That's exactly right, my husband said and leaned across her desk. Driving from Motovun you arrive first in Draguc and from Draguc the road goes on to Veli Mlun, that's of course on this side of Mali Mlun, but once you've driven through Mali Mlun you've got to be on your toes, my husband said to the woman behind the desk, do you follow me? You mustn't miss the small side-road to your right, aha, to the right, she said, to the right, my sweetie said, the thing to watch for is the sign which is not on the shoulder of the road where of course it should be, but almost in among the trees, that's to say, among the few trees that happen to be left in place, my sweetiepie said, do you follow, Good Lord, the woman behind the desk said, well, what I'm trying to say is that this sign is placed practically by the riverside on the right-hand side of the road where the Forestry Commission people from Buzet have cut down so many trees that the truffles no longer thrive there, imagine, the woman behind the desk said, a catastrophe, my sweetipie said, a real catastrophe, the effect on our country's economy is incalculable.

Though if you happen to come from the opposite direction, that's from here in Buzet, he went on, then you must first go through Vrh and Groznjan and be on the alert so that you don't turn right because that would take you towards Senj, so not towards Senj, the woman said,

RICHARD SWARTZ

under no circumstances towards Senj, my sweetiepie said, what you must do instead is to continue straight ahead and after half a kilometer or so you'll see the sign, though now on your left, of course.

What does the sign say, the woman behind the desk asked.

Pelegrin, my sweetie replied. It says Pelegrin on the sign.

Imagine, the woman behind the desk said, you make it sound so interesting.

Just straight up the hill, my husband said contentedly and looked around the office, taking in the folio-sized folders stacked on their sides or crammed into floor-to-ceiling shelves; the wall calendar from last year with a picture of a nude blonde, a tire round her waist; the fluttering spiders' webs in the corners near the ceiling; the crucifix with its bouquet of faded meadow flowers; the empty umbrella stand; the potted plants and the basin with a single cold-water faucet; and I could tell that he was in an excellent temper and delighted by all he saw.

Pelegrin, the woman sighed, well, Pelegrin, I'm afraid that means going up the ladder.

She got up from her chair at the desk and walked over to a ladder that I hadn't noticed when we entered, a ladder leaning against the wall on the right-hand side of the door, and by now my husband must have felt really at home and said in a loud, rather affected voice, sounding as if he were on stage, oh please, that is out of the question, I must protest, if anyone is to face this risk it's me, believe me, he cried and the woman must have been delighted with him, looking very pleased as he dashed forward to deal with the ladder. But with his bandaged hands he was not quite up to getting a proper grip or maybe the ladder was too heavy for him; anyway, the woman quite gently but firmly pushed him away.

Never mind, she said, I can cope with the ladder, and then she turned to me, imagine, she said, what a most obliging gentleman your husband is, and such an opportunity he could of course not let pass him by, now striking his chest with one bandaged hand and putting the other on his forehead, do not blame me, he exclaimed, turning a visit to check the Property Register into a theatrical performance, I would not have wished this, he cried, it is none of my doing, and the office lady tittered happily, but had no use either for him or for his bandaged hands. She hauled the ladder over to the wall behind me and climbed it, taking no further notice of my husband who was still performing on the floor below her, crying no, no, there must be no climbing unless I am the one going up that ladder, it is after all Juliet who must be on the balcony!

But the office lady no longer took any notice of him or did not grasp what he was talking about, tell your husband my name is Liljana, she called down from her perch on the ladder, but it sounded more like an amiable comment than a correction, and up there on the ladder her legs showed under the blue smock, two sturdy bare legs, chalky white but covered in black hairs, and without turning she handed down a thick, leather-bound folder that my husband blew the dust off, although this time he had to blow hard because the dust was real; and in order to find what we looked for meant quite a lengthy search, the pages of the folder being as brittle and translucent as the paper I had wrapped the cakes for Beppo in. It took us a long time turning the pages in the folder until we found Pelegrin, and almost as long again to locate the empty house, *our* house, as my sweetie calls it, but there it suddenly was, at the top of its own page with entries in red ink, the same *rosso romano* shade as the house itself, and all three of us bent over the folder and read: Property II a/25, owned by family Sirotic; confiscated May 1946; sold at public auction March 1954 to family Bartolovic; responsible owner B. C. Bartolovic, born Bartolo, deceased December 1962; above property thereupon transferred to the deceased's two daughters, Sonia Marija Zivkovic, nee Bartolovic, registered in Ulcinj, Montenegro, and Nina Baraldi, nee Bartolovic, now resident of Trieste, Italy, and an Italian citizen.

Confiscated, my sweetie whispered to me. What does it mean? Can we buy the house or not?

I straightened my back which had started to ache and hurt me again, smiled to the lady in the blue smock who had been so helpful, but who was now already turning the page in the folder, looking up and reading about quite different houses, and I said thank you very much, you've been most helpful.

Can we buy it, my husband asked again and now I'd

had enough and looked so sharply at him that the mere glance should make him realize how much I disapproved and that he really must hold his tongue, and then I said goodbye to the woman who had already forgotten about us, absorbed by reading the folder on Pelegrin and its neighborhood, and I pulled at my husband to make him leave the office with me.

The corridor outside was cool, we walked along it side by side in silence, our footsteps echoing under the vaults. But outside the heat had become almost unbearable, the polished paving stones burnt straight through the thin soles of my shoes, and to my husband I said that now I've had enough—all day yesterday I had to put up with your foul temper, I said, frankly speaking I don't believe any other woman would, and then you make fools of both of us in the village, but you don't stop at that and in there, even in the Land Surveyor's office, you're a nuisance; how many times have I told you that no one here understands your kind of humor, and he tried to say something in his own defense, but I really had had enough and told him that we now had to ask Franjo for advice.

Who's Franjo?

My lawyer, I replied. Franjo is the advocate who's been looking after my house and all my affairs here in Istria until I married someone who is not a local and understands nothing about property registers and even less about people who come from here, let alone the distinctions we make between confiscation and nationalization.

RICHARD SWARTZ

Is that an important difference, he asked, but I did not answer, I sometimes feel that nothing that is important to me matters the least bit to him.

I'm sorry, he mumbled, but not until we had got back into the car. The air in the car was even hotter than outside and driving back home to Pelegrin was unthinkable in such heat. It seemed better to try to see my lawyer while we were there in Buzet anyway, even though my sweetiepie was sitting silently next to me in the car now, not whistling anymore, but at least I didn't have to bother with his composers, neither with Léhar nor with Kálmán, and in such an atmosphere between us we drove all the way from the castle down into the town, not saying one word to each other, and during the entire drive my sweetie was just sitting there silent next to me, his arms crossed over his chest.

It was lunchtime by then and pointless to look in at Franjo's office, he would already have left his documents to go to his table in the restaurant round the corner. Every weekday the advocate sits at the table reserved for him, the table for the advocate's midday meal, the third table on the right-hand side counted from the doorway, and when I had pushed the door open and become used to the dim light inside, I spotted him at once sitting at the third on the right, with scraps of food still in front of him on two almost empty plates.

The advocate had finished his lunch. Now he was smoking a cigarette after his meal, and when he caught sight of me his face lit up and he waved to us, inviting us to come and sit at his table though he had not met my sweetiepie yet.

There's thunder in the air, advocate Franjo said without getting up from the table, nothing but storms and headaches all summer long. My husband was observing the lawyer, carefully noting how he looked, established at his regular table with a good view over the whole room, and I saw that my husband was still in a good mood, their minestrone is really excellent today, the advocate said, I can truly recommend it. But I had decided to get straight to the point and explained that we had not come for a meal.

Franjo, I said, do you remember that big empty house in Pelegrin?

He nodded.

My husband would like to buy it, I said, but all we know is that it belongs to a family called Bartolovic. Do you happen to know the owners? We must find the right people to negotiate with.

The advocate reached for a toothpick from the stand on the free table next to ours and started picking his teeth, holding his left hand in front of his mouth, and he muttered Bartolovic, Bartolovic, all very well, but which lot of Bartolovics? My dear lady, have you ever looked around the headstones in that cemetery of yours up in Pelegrin, he asked, and my husband was leaning forward to better catch what the advocate was saying.

There they all are, the advocate continued while still picking his teeth, Flegos, Martellis and all the Greblos, the German and Maier families, the Poropats and your Bartolovics, all of them are there, not more than six, maybe seven families, but just about enough to take over the entire cemetery in your Pelegrin. And to each family belongs a handful of graves, my dear lady, and mind you, I'm only counting headstones and crosses now, not all the names inscribed on them. I'm not talking about each one of those poor souls underground who've had to be satisfied with sharing a headstone or a cross with so many others. And you come here now to ask me if I know the Bartolovic family?

Yes, I said.

But whom do you specifically have in mind, he asked, and I saw that my sweetie found it hard to follow what the advocate was saying as he kept on picking his teeth behind his left hand, holding it in front of his mouth all the time he was talking.

Which one of the Bartolovic lot? Whom do you want to get hold of? Besides we could include the Bartolos, actually the same family. That's how it is up there in your Pelegrin, Bartolo or Bartolovic doesn't really matter. Politics, my dear lady! You certainly know how it goes, in our country politics gets into everything, the advocate said, even into the cemetery. Here we are born in one state and get buried in another without ever moving from the spot and as for the state itself, the lawyer said, it's as changeable as the weather; just when we've got used to the Italian flag the time has come for yet another one, a Yugoslav flag or a Croatian flag, anyway a flag with totally different colors from the one we were beginning to get used to. My dear lady, you should know what it's like! I personally know people who've had to take their hats off to each one of these flags, one after another, and that without ever traveling further than Draguc in this wide world of ours, the lawyer said. Believe me, the grave that'll be dug for you up there in your Pelegrin cemetery is the only thing you can count on though God only knows what's the best emblem to pick for your headstone, a cross or the red partisan star, he said, which one would give you a better chance to rest in peace for a decent length of time. Who can really tell? If the dead had better stick to the Church and the Bible or put their trust in being a member of the Communist Party? And while they were still alive it was just as hard for them to make the right choice, he said, some joined the Italians, others preferred to tie a Croatian cravat around the neck and dash about writing *We Want Tito* on the walls, or at least they did until the partisans turned up and drank all their wine and stole their money, the advocate said. Up there in Pelegrin you've still got Tito in red paint on your walls, isn't that so, my dear lady?

And Franjo was right: the walls of both the little shop and the house opposite are still daubed with slogans like *We Want Tito*, and nobody has taken the trouble to paint them over even though we have a new flag by now and communism has vanished; and I told Franjo that he was quite right, but it surprised me that he knew about our Pelegrin in so much detail.

Still that's nothing compared to Veli Mlun, said the advocate, in Veli Mlun it's not red paint but blood, a whole wall covered with dried blood, right on the spot where the partisans shot the local priest, and by now the advocate had stopped picking his teeth and was wiping his forehead with a paper napkin. In the end it's all the same, he said, and my sweetie nodded as if he had understood. But it must be said that blood is worse than paint. Blood is the worst and there is no insurance against bloodshed, the advocate said, waving his left hand as if he tried to swat a fly, insurance against what, my sweetie asked, once there's blood on the floor there is no help, Franjo said, who didn't seem to have heard my husband's question. No help at all! Never mind that some of them called themselves Bartolo and others Bartolovic so that the family would at least have something left in the bank, come what may, regardless of which flag was run up the flagpole, the advocate said. Still, you can get shot anyway.

I thought that maybe you knew something about the owners, I said to him.

I have already told you all I know, advocate Franjo replied.

Something about the owners of the empty house.

But which one do you want? Bartolovic, Bartolovic, he muttered irritably, there are any number of them up there. There's not a single soul in Pelegrin who's not more or less a Bartolovic and if you don't spot one straightaway, just pick any Flego or Maier and scratch his surface for a little bit and soon you'll get to a Bartolovic.

The whole churchyard is just one big family grave, dear lady, and that's how it's been for more than two hundred years. What more can I say? Just go ahead and read the inscriptions on the stones. And now you want one specific Bartolovic, the one who owns the empty house, the advocate said, shaking his head.

Yes, I said.

But every single one of them has owned that house in one way or another or, come to think of it, it's the other way around, it's the house in Pelegrin that's owned the family for the last two hundred years, the advocate said, and the house has got rid of every single one of its owners, Bartolo or Bartolovic makes no difference. One by one the owners disappeared from the house and never came back and against this kind of thing there's no help, neither a contract nor a life insurance, the advocate said, and believe me, none of the owners ever meant anything to the house. If a Bartolo or a Bartolovic, each and every one sooner or later ended up buried under a stone in the Pelegrin cemetery while the house still stays above ground: Isn' t that so my dear lady? The house still stands up there on the hill while every Bartolo or Bartolovic who's ever lived in it is dead and gone with only the worms in the cemetery for company, isn't that so, the advocate asked. And once in the churchyard soil the last differences between us disappear and people like me, that is, a human being with a degree in law, are only interested in those who are still above ground. The law is only for those still alive. For such people my office can still do something, provided they can pay my fees.

We would be satisfied with just one Bartolovic as long as he's alive, my sweetie said, who seemed not to have understood everything Franjo had been saying, as the advocate had spent quite some time picking his teeth, his left hand hiding both his mouth and many of his words.

My husband has set his heart on buying the house, I said.

That's not a course of action I can recommend, Franjo said, examining my husband across the table. If I've understood matters correctly, he's not a Bartolovic. Not even a Bartolo.

I can't see why that should matter, my husband said kindly, still in a good mood.

Of course you don't, the advocate said. How could you?

Again he wiped his forehead, using the paper napkin on which was written *Buzet Pizza Prima Italiana*.

Listen, he said, that house and the Bartolovic family have belonged together for two hundred years and now you want to come along and change everything, just because the house happens to be empty and strikes your fancy for some reason. But what do you really know about the house? That it's empty? Indeed it is. But before it became empty there was always a Bartolo or a Bartolovic living in it. Everyone around here has lost track by now of how many generations back the relationship goes or why it started in the first place, all we know is that the owner has always been either a Bartolo or a Bartolovic. Do you see what I mean? And as far as the house is concerned it makes no difference that people don't know the exact number of owners or who came after whom, all we need to know is that it always was a Bartolo or a Bartolovic, nothing further is called for. This is all we need to know about the house and it actually simplifies matters that the owners cannot be distinguished from each other any more, advocate Franjo said. For two hundred years now it's as if the house has had only one single owner, not several, and whether the house stays empy or not doesn't really matter either, not the slightest, he said, and if your imagination can't cope with that single owner you can always try imagining nobody at all, a house without owner. One owner or no owner at all is in this case all the same, the advocate said and looked first at me and then at my husband. One or no one makes no difference. Not here in Istria. That's how things are here with us. What matters for us about the house is only the point of view. That's the beginning and end of it. There is no other way to go about it. Believe me, the advocate said, I give you my word as a lawyer.

We will of course do what you will advise us, my husband said, but the advocate did not listen.

Just don't think that this owner or non-owner can ever be replaced by some new and utterly unknown person, the advocate said, someone who's neither a Bartolo nor a Bartolovic. That's impossible, totally out of the question. In this country blood is of the utmost importance, the advocate said, *ius sanguinis* reigns here, he added, and there is already too much blood associated with that empty house, but Bartolo blood or Bartolovic blood, not yours. Is that not so, my dear lady, Franjo asked, turning to me, you certainly realize that I'm speaking to you in confidence, but this must be properly understood and that's why I am saying this to you not so much as your lawyer but more as your friend, if you'll permit me, Franjo said, although I had never thought of him as anything other than my advocate, and would have preferred him to just supply the address of the owner of the house instead of rambling around the cemetery in Pelegrin where addresses are pointless in any case.

Are you sure you wouldn't like something to eat, Franjo asked. Around us, the other guests had started on the dessert of the day, except for those who were smoking their first or maybe second cigarette after the meal, the risotto too was excellent today, Franjo said, and once again I explained that we weren't hungry, that we had just come to consult him, and then went on telling him how grateful we were for his time and especially for his regarding me more as a friend than a client.

That goes without saying, the advocate said, looking out over the restaurant, pleased with himself. Indeed, my dear lady, we all think very highly of you here and therefore your husband is also welcome to join me at my table. You are simply one of us although it's not quite true, Rijeka is after all situated on the other side of the Ucka, but not even you can deny that this man is a stranger, said advocate Franjo and pointed at my husband.

As far as we Istrians are concerned, your husband is a complete stranger, the advocate said. A nobody. As a true friend of yours, my dear lady, I must allow myself to be forthright. This man is a stranger, the advocate said and pointed at my husband again, something that might change only after generations and therefore it's out of the question that such a person should buy a house here, and not any old house on top of it, but that empty Bartolovic or Bartolo house up in Pelegrin, and by now Franjo had turned and was speaking to my husband. Impossible, he said. Totally out of the question. Forget that house. It's not for sale.

Franjo fell silent for a moment or two and then looked at me, wiping his face again with the paper napkin.

You may wonder, he said, if I'm not now pleading against my own interests. As a member of the legal profession I should surely be ready to act on behalf of my client. Yes. That is true. But I've taken the liberty of speaking to you as your friend, my dear lady, not as your lawyer. Trust me! Your husband will find it impossible to buy that house, it's quite out of the question. Anyway, what would he want it for? Here in our country buying something would give him no special rights over what he had bought. Of course, he's free to buy what he likes, but what he has bought would not necessarily from now on belong to him and remain his property. Buying alters nothing except in a purely formal sense, on paper that is.

But, my dear lady, you know all this as well as I do, and thinking about it, what can we truly call our own in this life, the advocate asked and sighed, apparently contemplating his own words and especially pleased with the last passage, though to me his ideas seemed more like a philosopher's than those of a lawyer, and I suddenly felt very uncomfortable sitting there on my chair; also here, inside the restaurant, it was far too hot. My dress was sticking to the seat and sweat gleamed on both sides of the advocate's pale nose.

Everything in this life is either stolen or on loan, he said abruptly, looking at my husband. The worst criminals are those who are unaware of their own motives, and end up behind bars not understanding why they committed their crimes, and to me as a lawyer not the criminal but his motive is the only thing of interest in the long run and as far as you are concerned, Franjo said to my husband, I couldn't care less. You don't interest me at all, but your motive does. Why would a stranger like you want to buy the empty house in Pelegrin? What possible motive can you have, he asked, but rather than giving my sweetie time to answer the question, the advocate went on to remind him that one day he'd be carried out of the house and end up in the cemetery like all those before him, though resting in foreign soil, and not in his own, so that you risk being dug up like potatoes at any time, the advocate said, but all this is no concern of mine, of course, he continued, what interests me is simply your motive for getting involved with that house. Nothing else is of any interest to me in my capacity as a lawyer since you're neither a Bartolovic nor a Bartolo. It's your motive alone that I want to understand, advocate Franjo said, and then, turning to me, my dear lady, just try to imagine how it feels to occupy yourself all your life with the affairs of people who are of no interest whatsoever to you if it hadn't been for their motives, but these people themselves have no idea of their motives or at least refuse to speak about them. Can you imagine such a life? No, you can't. But that's how I have spent my entire life, advocate Franjo said, then explaining to us how all his own time had been stolen from him while he in court was occupied restoring from criminals what they had stolen from others; while I was in court pleading on their behalf they stole my life away, the advocate said. At the end all my time was totally swallowed up by their thefts and racketeering. That's how my life has been spent, the advocate said and then, turning to my husband, he started to explain how nowadays up-to-date crimes can be so cunningly crafted that the victim doesn't even notice that he has been robbed, and how the police can rarely be bothered to investigate crimes of this kind, crimes leaving no trace or even evidence that they have really happened; anyway, there's not much point in reporting crimes of this sort to the police, and the same goes for my life, the advocate said. When I turn around and look back, there's nothing there. All those criminals have stolen my life away, advocate Franjo said, and so, my dear lady, he said and turned to me, I've simply made up my mind to stay

RICHARD SWARTZ

alive a little longer. I've no intention to leave this life totally empty-handed just because those criminals stole all
my time, he said and sighed again. And I am afraid that it
is you, the decent clients, who have to pay for the time
stolen from your lawyers, and now you see why it must
be so. But there's no fee to be paid for motives. That's
why they almost always remain undetected and you seem
to be one of those who have hidden your motive skill-
fully enough to really interest me, Franjo said and looked
at my husband.

What's your real reason for wanting to buy that house?

I like it, my husband said.

There you are, Franjo said and now he was talking
to me. What did I tell you? I've worked in the legal profession in this town for forty years. And what have I
learned? That people around here cannot even be bothered to have proper motives for what they do. They prefer to lie. Our dear lady here can confirm that I'm not
exaggerating, Franjo said, pointing at me. But the law has
simply no place for exaggeration. For a good career in
the courtroom, what you need is the ability to stick to
facts, and a well-padded behind, the advocate said and
pushed the two empty plates further away on the table.
Well, my dear lady, wouldn't it be a good idea to take a
look at the menu after all?

But the midday break, a time of rest in Buzet, was
coming to an end. Just a moment ago the quiet restaurant
had felt sleepy, but at once all the guests were getting
ready to leave and seemed agitated, as if suddenly an

abyss had opened in the middle of the afternoon and taken them all by complete surprise. All the tables were demanding their bills and advocate Franjo also insisted on paying, and in this chaos there was no room for anything but clamoring for the two waiters and when calling wasn't enough, trying to catch their attention in some other way, and the advocate was tapping his spoon against the edge of a plate; the air was full of calls and noise, all the guests were intent on only this one thing while making as much noise as possible, but meanwhile one of the waiters had disappeared into the kitchen and the other one turned his back on the customers, busying himself at the blackboard hanging on the wall just to the right of the front door, wiping it with a damp cloth to remove the chalked list of the main course and dessert of the day, and I asked myself if it might not after all have been a mistake to consult my lawyer over lunch at the table reserved for him, even though he'd been addressing us as if arguing a case in court, not talking to us in the local restaurant. But what might have led to further judicious discussion in court, here got lost in all the noise: tinkling glasses, knives and spoons clattering on plates, chattering across the tables as dissatisfied guests complained loudly about the waiter who had failed to serve up the final orders, placed more than a quarter of an hour ago.

But by now it was too late for a crème caramel or a piece of cake, and the advocate seemed as irritated as everyone else, *ius sanguinis*, that's all they understand, Franjo muttered, I'm the only one in this town who's interested in motives, but my husband who's not from these parts leaned forward and said to Franjo you're wrong, you underestimate the significance of exaggeration.

What, the advocate said.

You talked about exaggeration before, my husband said.

Did I?

You did, my husband told him, and sometimes it's precisely exaggeration that provides the crucial motive, something you lawyers normally fail to take into account, so to speak *per definitionem*—what did you say, the advocate asked, holding his cupped right hand behind his ear and leaning forward over the table—*per definitionem*, my sweetie repeated and Franjo nodded coldly and sat back in his chair. Someone like you, my husband said, is bound to underestimate the motivational importance of exaggeration simply by being who you are, and I wondered where he had gathered all this knowledge of the legal profession. But, my dear sir, when you consider the rest of us, ordinary people like me with no qualifications in the law, my husband said, you'll find that we love exaggeration. We let our emotions rule us. Our desires are boundless and you and your paragraphs can do nothing about it. But how could the legal mind grasp that the law is the enemy of every passion? If we get a chance to exaggerate we will do it, my husband said to Franjo, we love exaggeration precisely because within it lies our only freedom, my husband insisted, and the advocate mumbled something I did not catch.

Didn't you've say you had forty years experience? Well, then I am sure that you'll already have heard what I'm telling you now, my husband said to the advocate, who in the middle of the turmoil in the restaurant inclined his head to the right, just a fraction, so he seemed to be listening to my husband, though I believe this was just a polite gesture, the advocate was in fact preoccupied with checking the bill that the waiter had now put in front of him; with his eyes half closed he was going through the items, time and again nodding his head, barely noticeable twitches, or maybe his head was just wobbling, but still so that it looked as if he were ticking off the lunch bill—a glass of grappa, a hot main course with salad, a glass of wine and that crème caramel for dessert—but encouraged by what he took to be Franjo's interest, my sweetie repeated what he had already been saying about passion and exaggeration; ordinary people like us would be lost without our exaggerations, he said, in exaggeration alone lies our salvation. Just give us half a chance and we will cross any line drawn up to keep us in place, whether dictated by law or the inertia of the heart makes no difference.

Yes, yes, the advocate said and nodded, but as if he weren't listening, and maybe I alone was taking in what my sweetie had to say, although I didn't understand it all and thought this poetic language must be wasted on a lawyer. But feeling that my husband's words, poetic and somehow shy, were about something else, about something that had to do with himself and not with the law, I took it all to my heart.

It is all very well for you to speak about sticking to the facts, he said to Franjo, who by now had paid the bill and was carefully pushing his change over the edge of the tabletop into his cupped hand, and then putting both the coins and the bill away in his jacket pocket, you lawyers just keep shoving your facts down our throats, my husband said, as if you thought your paragraphs had any power over us. There you are with all your paragraphs and regulations and all that fine print on the back of the contract you use for penning us in behind what you think is the right side of the fence. In the name of decency and the law, of course. No exaggerations permitted! And that's the way you really think we'll lead our lives, and even insisting that we pay you in return, my husband said, but advocate Franjo was shaking his head, you don't understand a thing, he said.

Really, my sweetie protested. So I don't understand, is that what you think?

All exaggeration ends with blood, the advocate replied coldly, and in a way I believe that Franjo was right; my sweetie was now really talking about blood, but his own.

From the depths of his heart he had been speaking about his feelings, but in an almost lyrical way, for in his case that was the kind of day it was; my husband was still in a good mood and I was listening carefully to every one of his words even though I have no legal training and wasn't really convinced that my husband and I should buy the empty house in Pelegrin but what he had been speaking about had, indeed, little to do with the house. His mind was set on other things and I believe my sweetie was talking only to me, not to the advocate, but since Franjo was in our company and this was the very first time they had met my husband stuck to the law; out of politeness, I think, but to me it made no difference, none at all, I felt that every word was meant for me and not for advocate Franjo, and I was wishing I could help my sweetie. At his most helpless he seems unable to express what's in his heart and this was now the case, he was speaking to me about his love for me in front of an advocate, not about the house business any longer, our actual errand, but that's also the reason why I am so fond of him, his way of being so incredibly awkward sometimes and shy, now forcing himself to talk about legal paragraphs and contracts and not about the two of us, but speaking in such a lyrical way that I would have liked to show him that I had understood him, that I knew that what he was saying had nothing to do with legalities, not even with the empty house in Pelegrin, *our* house as he calls it, but that he in front of my lawyer was declaring his love for me, nothing else.

But I couldn't. I was not able to let him know how I felt, just as my husband now wasn't able to talk about his own feelings but resorted to legalities and this saddened me a little, even though I know he can't manage any other way, and meanwhile advocate Franjo was shaking his head; time and again he was shaking his head, but by now it was my husband's many failures to understand he was ticking off.

You understand nothing, Franjo said. Not even a contract will help you. The house is not meant for you. Forget it. The house is not for sale. *Basta.*

Then Franjo told me that he had some documents to do with an insurance policy of mine and he wanted me to collect them from his office. Outside the restaurant the town looked gray as ashes and seemed to be dissolving in the heat. Above us on the hill the fort was shuddering like the crème caramel on the dessert plates in the restaurant, and all three of us tried to keep in the shade of the houses. But before setting out Franjo wanted to buy a newspaper from the kiosk at the stop for the Rijeka bus where I usually collect my mother, and although it is not far from the restaurant the advocate soon was panting, it sounded as if he couldn't get enough air, despite the heat advocate Franjo was wearing a woolen suit and vest.

Always dressed with total disregard for the season the advocate was now panting and sweating, the sweat was pouring down his face and neck, but once the advocate hadn't had this neck for his head, once his head had seemed to emerge directly from his small body, his big head sitting between his shoulders without a neck to it, so that over the years he always had been looking up at his clients and the citizens of Buzet with his unmoving, hard stare directed at everyone from below, a way of looking at things and people particularly advantageous in a courtroom. But as the years passed the center of gravity in his lawyer's body must have shifted from shoulders and head down towards his waist and stomach; on his thin legs Franjo was now maneuvering a body more and more dominated by a belly which hadn't been there before, and as more of his body shifted towards waist and belly, more had retreated from the places where it used to be, so that the advocate, now on his way to buy a newspaper after finishing his lunch, was equipped with a neck he hadn't had before, but not enough of one, too frail to hold up the advocate's large head wobbling from side to side as he, keeping in the shade of the houses, was tottering along on his thin legs towards the kiosk where he used to pick up his daily paper to read about the latest news; but his unstable head made him seem uncertain and indecisive, certainly not to his advantage in court, and I couldn't help remembering what they're saying about advocate Franjo in Buzet these days—that nothing is as it used to be, except that the advocate in the winter still dresses as if it were summer and in the summer wears a woolen suit with a vest—but also that he no longer wins his court cases and his office is so chaotic he's always losing documents there, even originals; that and nowadays spending more time over his lunch table in the Grotta Azzurra than in his own office, that the advocate doesn't earn his income from clients' fees anymore, but gets money from Italian lawyers in Trieste in exchange for providing them with entries copied from the Istrian

Personal and Property Register, documentation that is used on the Italian side of the border by Italian lawyers in Italian courts to extract cash in the form of state benefits from Rome, damages and war pensions; these are the stories making the rounds in Buzet, and also that with the advocate's help some Italians have even gotten their hands on empty houses on our side of the border.

Advocate Franjo is thought to be on the slippery slope financially, but I haven't taken much notice of the gossip about him, people often say what is not necessarily true or could be true only if one includes what they do *not* say; but in Buzet people still took the trouble to greet the advocate as he walked from the Grotta Azzurra to the newspaper kiosk in that afternoon heat.

The barber on the corner came out from his shop to greet Franjo and the advocate greeted him with a bow, or maybe it was just his head wobbling on the neck he previously did not have, but which ever since it showed up had been adding to his reverses in court. The barber greeted Franjo and so did the two sisters from Kaldir who were sitting in the shade on the bench by the bus stop, but behind his back the sisters were laughing at him and I saw how the barber snipped the air a couple of times with his scissors, that he too made fun of the advocate behind his back; and to everyone he met on the way to the newspaper kiosk Franjo had something to say, things like don't forget about Tuesday, or so school is already over today, or how is your mother, advocate Franjo said, please give my regards to dear Maria, each time bowing to the person he was addressing; and also the Albanian who owns the greengrocer's stall near the newspaper kiosk greeted the advocate, that stall where the Albanian's daughter sells potatoes and bananas although she is barely tall enough to reach the counter, while her father spends his days near the stall, standing in the shade of the large chestnut tree fiddling with his key-ring, keeping an eye on the time; and both of them greeted the advocate and so, like everybody else, did the lady in the kiosk who greeted him behind her pane in spite of the heat in her glassed-in booth, large dark stains showed on her dress under the armpits and in the fold between her breasts, everybody was greeting, but the Albanian was mocking the advocate behind his back.

Please put a paper to the side for me tomorrow as usual, Franjo said, his large head wobbling from side to side, and while everybody had greeted him I had seen for myself that no one had anything more than just that greeting to offer the advocate.

Not one of them had stopped for a moment to speak to him about the weather or the sudden heat, let alone to discuss something that really mattered, and the insurance documents that he asked me to collect from his office were of no real importance either. Only out of politeness had I agreed to come along with him, maybe also from feeling sorry for him, and for my parents' sake, my parents who had known the old lawyer since way back, and not even to myself could I explain why I had told my husband that this meeting was so important and why we had to consult advocate Franjo in particular. No explanation came to mind, especially not after my husband's performance in the Land Surveyor's office where my sweetiepie had behaved quite outrageously, making us both look ridiculous, but the distinction between nationalization and confiscation had to be discussed with someone qualified in law, in other words with Franjo, the only lawyer I know and my only contact with the legal profession in Buzet, although a lawyer with fading reputation whose walk from the restaurant to the newspaper kiosk at the bus stop and from there back to his office was no longer the stroll of a well-respected advocate meeting his neighbors and clients, but of someone being pilloried by the inhabitants of a small provincial town that had already written him off; and Franjo's head was wobbling from one side to another as if from every direction he had been beaten with sticks as he walked along, the blows striking his head and shoulders again and again. From one side to another the advocate's head was wobbling under the blows, a large shaking head belonging to a lonely old man, but it was only after having started to lose his court cases and with them his legal standing that Franjo had been written off by the town; before that no one here would have ignored or made mock of him.

Only his failures in the courtroom had brought him down and because they would never have dared to give him the cold shoulder before, everyone was eager to do it now. People in Buzet wanted to show the old advocate that they were perfectly aware that he'd never been anything but a hopeless lawyer, a disaster for anyone hoping to get a sentence in their favor in court, and that for the last forty years they had come to him only because there had been nobody else to turn to with their claims for justice and financial rewards, that this had been the only reason for using his services, but then losing their cases as well as their cash thanks to his boundless incompetence though you might have been warned, for what kind of advocate would turn up in court wearing a short-sleeved shirt in the middle of winter?

But no one dared to tell him any of this, and Franjo kept greeting each and every one of them, including those who later laughed at him behind his back.

Year after year he had carried on greeting them all, after all this was his hometown, this town full of people who after forty years had started to laugh at him secretly, a very old man on very thin legs, and once buried in the Buzet cemetery nothing would be left of advocate Franjo but the town's recollections. People would recall how every day he would walk from his office to his lunch in the restaurant and then a couple of hours later to the newspaper kiosk, where his order—a pack of Moravas and a copy of *Glas Istre*—would be waiting for him, day after day for as long as anyone in the town could remember, and how he then would walk back to his office, piled high with court papers; people would remember nothing but this, and how during his daily walk he always had been treated with proper respect and sympathy, as was his due as advocate Franjo Laginja, son to Dr. Ivan Laginja

and his wife Antonia, née Stuparich-Zernatto, the foremost practitioner of the legal vocation in the court of
Buzet.

Many times I had of course visited his office, no more
than two tiny rooms with a connecting door, but my
husband looked astonished, as if he had been expecting
at least a brass plate engraved with the advocate's name
and office hours, all in big black letters and numbers. On
the desk stood a computer with an undulating pattern on
the screen, blue waves slowly rising and falling, as if the
screen might have been showing weather fronts or the
Northern lights that my sweetie sometimes talks about
and I've seen on television once, and in the office it was
almost as hot as it had been in the street. The advocate,
who seemed to treat the office as his home, at once sank
down in the armchair behind his desk, pressed a button
on the computer with a trembling, white finger so that it
shut down and the blue waves disappeared from the
screen, and then he said he would like to get the two of
us a cup of coffee, but first had to rest his legs, and pleadingly he looked at my husband.

Please, be so kind and lift my legs up on the desk, he
asked, but both at the same time, if you would, and my
husband lifted both the advocate's legs up on the desk
and then carefully put his feet down among the papers
and court documents on the desktop.

Thank you, the advocate whispered, that's much better, and he started massaging his legs, moaning and mumbling to himself. There, there, he mumbled, there, there, believe it or not, but it must be the thunderstorm. I can feel the thunder in my legs long before it reaches Motovun, sometimes several days ahead.

Now, from Pelegrin you can see Motovun, can't you, he asked, looking up from the armchair at my husband while carrying on kneading his legs, not caring that he wasn't alone in his office, as if massaging your legs in the presence of visitors is more or less the same as raising your hat to greet them, at least when you are in your own place. The advocate had almost closed his eyes. Tears were trickling from both of them and his head was trembling almost imperceptibly on his neck, rather like a float bobbing up and down on the surface of the water while the fisherman is watching it, feeling uncertain if it is just a breeze from the shore or a fish that's nibbling the worm and soon will pull the float down into the depths, and I started worrying about the advocate falling asleep in the chair behind his desk, thinking that the lunch and the walk to get his paper while wearing a woolen suit in that afternoon heat together with our visit might have been too much for the old man, and I wanted to tell him that there was no hurry: the papers from the insurance company could wait. After all we go down to Buzet pretty often to do some shopping, but of what I intended to say I said nothing. Really, this is my big flaw, the fact that I only afterwards tend to realize how much better it would be to say out loud what I want to say but never do, because I always feel that it might not be the right time. That's exactly what you should have said, people who know me and wish me well advise me when later on I tell them about what I had planned to say, but did not get round to at the time, and before I had opened my mouth Franjo looked up and asked my sweetiepie about his sleeping habits—if he gets up early in the morning.

Do you sleep well at night, the advocate asked.

At my age one tends to wake up early in the morning, he said without waiting for an answer. My dear lady, you must forgive me, Franjo said, looking up at me from his chair, but I have reached the age when one has to get up every so often, not just in the morning but also several times during the night. Not for long and not for anything of real importance, no, nothing of the kind my dear lady, but long enough to do what has to be done in the toilet, because if I don't the rest of my time in bed before it starts to get light outside becomes rather painful. In the end the only thing I long for is to get up and out of bed. But all this dashing about, in and out of the bedroom all night, really means that I need my sleep although it doesn't come easily at all, he said, at my age proper sleep seems totally out of the question, so once I've been up to do what I must I remain there in bed on my back doing nothing at all, even though I'm wide awake and quite unable to fall asleep again.

But you are still a young man, Franjo said to my sweetie, I'm sure you find it easy to sleep all night through and almost certainly you wake up late in the morning with a hard-on, the advocate said, and I had expected him to turn to me with another apology, but no, not this time.

Instead he was looking curiously at my husband who was smiling as he met the old man's eyes, a smile that could be suggesting that the advocate's assumptions were quite correct, though if truth be told, I would have a thing or two to say about all this too. But I did not open my mouth; as usual, I did not present my point of view.

At my age . . . the advocate began again, but suddenly stopped speaking.

What is there to add, he said after a moment of silence. I have my lunch. Grotta Azzurra. Every day. A glass of wine or two at most. And a grappa after the meal. Knock on wood, my head is still clear. The crossword puzzle in the paper, my dear lady. The crossword puzzle and the obituaries. That's all. As for sleeping, well no, I don't sleep any longer. And the rest? Aches and pains. Breaking wind. What's left of my body seems to consist of wind, nothing but wind.

My dear lady, your old friend has turned into wind and not much else, Franjo said to me.

Well, well, the advocate said with a sigh and started kneading his legs again. His feet were resting in their black shoes on the desktop, shoes with heels that raised the advocate off the ground and made him a few centimeters taller, pointy black shoes of a kind I had not seen since my father's funeral and more suitable for a coffee house than for a courtroom.

Suddenly Franjo turned back to my husband.

What's your name again?

My sweetie told him.

Aha, the advocate said and his eyes had closed again. And with a name like that you want to buy a house in these parts?

I thought it must have been the heat that made him start speaking about the empty house again, now that he was back in his own office.

But we could always buy the house in my wife's name, my sweetie said and he was right, his own name had nothing whatsoever to do with the house. But the advocate did not reply, only rubbed his hands, his two pale and almost transparent hands were sliding across each other, back and forth, and from time to time the fingers would twist together so that the hands appeared to either clutch or caress each other. His fingers were moving in and out, exchanging places, curling round and sliding across each other so that I couldn't make up my mind if hands like his, which kept moving so smoothly that you could hardly keep the left and the right apart, would be of advantage for advocate Franjo or not when he set about arguing his case in court. But the thing he did with his hands must have been a habit acquired during all those years in the courtroom, a habit he no longer could do anything about, not even now when he no longer won his cases, and his two hands were in constant motion, over and across each other, making it impossible to keep track of them or to count the fingers on the advocate's hands, if you wanted to.

Bartolovic, he said to himself. Always a Bartolovic or a Bartolo. Yes, yes. It's all the same.

The advocate sighed and shook his head, my husband stayed silent and I too did not speak, and yet my sweetie was right; my name would be better than his. His name wouldn't get us very far, it would take us nowhere, a name like his is useless here in Istria. The advocate said nothing and outside a speeding motorbike roared past. Then the street fell silent again.

Would you, please, take my shoes off, Franjo suddenly asked my husband.

I have a pair of soft slippers ready right here under my desk, the advocate said, and my husband leaned forward and began to undo the laces on his shoes. Carefully he pulled Franjo's shoes off his feet, first the left and then the right while the advocate was moaning, I think not so much because the heat had made his feet swell and ache so that they hurt when the shoes were pulled off, but out of pure delight, and although both my husband's hands were bandaged he managed to take off the shoes so gently that nothing he did caused any pain, and I recalled how the two men had smiled at each other when they spoke of the state in which a man might wake up in the morning, and still I said nothing; but my sweetie's gentleness towards the old man was touching, reminding me of how he sometimes in the morning massages me firmly but softly, starting with my shoulders and all the way down along my spine, then up again the same way, utter bliss when my back is aching so badly I cannot get out of bed, yes, my husband on such mornings shows a care and thoughtfulness one perhaps wouldn't expect of him, and then my husband took the slippers from their place under the desk and put them down in front of the advocate's chair. Gently he lifted both Franjo's legs off the desktop, lowered them and pushed the small feet into the slippers, patterned in checks the size of stamps, rather like the advocate's woolen suit though the colors, small green squares alternating with red, were different.

My dear lady, this heat will kill us all one day, you can see for yourself how poorly I'm feeling, Franjo said. And if the heat doesn't get us then the cold will, our terrible northern wind, cutting through flesh and bones, chilling us to the marrow and reminding us of all the internal organs we're usually unaware of because our bodies keep them bundled away and out of sight. But in the winter they're aching all the time, and let me give you a piece of advice, just a single one, my dear lady! Don't try to fight nature. Neither the wind from the north nor the heat in the summer!

Sooner or later you will die anyhow, the advocate said and sounded as if he demanded some kind of order in how people die, for quiet deaths in properly made beds, but then he apologized; I too will die, no getting around that, he said, but if there's one thing I've learnt in all these years it's that when life flows one way there is no use trying to bend it into another direction. Resistance only speeds up what's inevitable anyhow. But it's only late in life that I've come to realize this.

A H o u s e i n I s t r i a 75

My dear lady, are you afraid of the dark? Of what might be there beyond it? Or does it frighten you even more to think that there might be nothing at all on the other side? My dear lady, people die so messily. They cling to life as if they believed that doing so could keep death at bay, not understanding that wasting all that energy clinging on to life kills what they might have of talent and joy. And as for myself, the advocate said, when I dig my heels in and try to resist all that happens is that I lose my breath and become dizzy, and sleep is of course something I don't have in any circumstances, least of all at night, but if I resisted and tried to set myself up against nature for any length of time I would drop dead immediately. At least much sooner than could be expected in my case, the advocate said, and Dr. Kontic is not constantly warning me against too much cholesterol for nothing.

He's advising me against blood sausage and pork of any kind. Leave it out, Dr. Kontic tells me, at your age you must watch your cholesterol levels, but I always eat blood sausage in the autumn, every autumn this side of the war, for more than half a century now, and often even during the war when there was little food to be had, so how could I be expected to miss out on blood sausage? But Dr. Kontic has already forbidden pork rinds and spit-roasted suckling pig, a catastrophe, my dear lady, you know what it's like everywhere between Zagreb and Istria, all the way down to us over Gorski Kotor people enjoy nothing better than grilling a suckling pig or a lamb, of late they're even doing young chickens, all sorts of animals, as if they had nothing better to do or think about than grilling and eating, the advocate said. Just imagine! They're lining up along the road with their grills so that sometimes you're forced to roll up the car windows to keep yourself under control, and guard against that smell of grilled suckling pig, well, my dear lady, don't we know the story, always the nose, it's always our noses that lead us into perdition, also when liver and gall bladder and heart are about to pack it up already, in fact all my internal organs are telling me to behave, and Dr. Kontic has already forbidden lard along with every other kind of animal fat, and a grilled pig's head—I can't even think of it. Not to mention fatty poultry like geese or ducks! All forbidden, not worth thinking about, so that I must drive all the way down to Gorski Kotor with the car windows rolled up even on the hottest days, on that stretch of road I have to take a stand against both weather and nature itself, my dear lady, for the sake of my health, to stop my nose leading me into temptation. So, there you are, and for me there is nothing much to look forward to anymore, and if Dr. Kontic would forbid me also blood sausage I really wouldn't know what to do, so for heaven's sake, not blood sausage too, and although you are a woman and like most women probably stick to a different kind of food I'm sure you know what I'm talking about, also your poor father, God bless the Colonel, the advocate went on, looking at me with his runny eyes, the Colonel also valued real food with peaches and cherries afterwards, and if his doctor would have also denied him blood sausage after already having forbidden almost every other part of the beast, well, my dear lady, I really don't know what he would have done, your poor father who never went anywhere without his pistol, such were the times, my dear lady, a handsome man and a partisan, I mean your poor father, but I can't imagine how he would have managed without his blood sausage, the advocate said, and I've been told he didn't take his holster and pistol off even at Christmas, your poor dear mother, always busy as she was with church matters, and especially at Christmastime, even though your blessed father had forbidden her having anything whatsoever to do with religion, little baby Jesus was no concern of his, the advocate said, though it's impossible to think of the church up there in Trsat without your dear mother and the three wise men who arrived too late in Bethlehem, too late for Christmas, I mean, and it's really a mystery how marriages ever lasted the way they did back in the old days, no one can explain it, although I suppose women could always love their children or Jesus, so much simpler that way, a more manageable form of love, my dear lady, no bruises, no weeping over the kitchen sink, the advocate said, and of course the colonel was always busy in the service of the Party, all the time taking his pistol apart and greasing all the bits and pieces before putting the whole thing together again, yes, that's the kind of marriage it was, but thank God communism came to an end so that your dear mother can go to church as often as she likes now without being frightened of her husband, isn't that so, my dear lady? But by then he was already dead, a sad fact but there you are, maybe just as well, the Colonel would never have put up with all that happened afterwards, thank God he didn't live to see it, I mean what happened to his communism and your dear mother forever in church these days, Christmas or no Christmas, without having to ask for permission.

It would have broken the poor colonel's heart, the advocate said, and it's more than likely that he hung on to his pistol after retiring, he kept watching out for enemies of our state although retired, so there's no telling what would have happened if your father were still alive, I mean what he would do or not do, advocate Franjo said, with or without his pistol, but thank God he is already dead and gone, he added, our poor old Colonel never had to face our present times.

My husband never met my father, I told Franjo, but this piece of information seemed to make no impression on him.

None of us escapes his fate, the advocate said and shook his head. I know I can't cheat death, my dear lady, not even by giving up on blood sausage. Not even following Dr. Kontic' orders can prevent my death, but giving up on blood sausage would make me the laughing stock of the Grotta Azzurra. They would start making fun of me in the restaurant. Jokes would be made at my expense, my dear lady, behind my back, naturally. They'd say that advocate Laginja is trying for eternal life, he's stopped eating blood sausage. Look at the advocate, they would say, that's his new way of life, no blood sausage. I know them well enough, my dear lady, that's what they would say, word for word, the advocate insisted, but at my age all change is damaging and I have the intention to live at least a little longer, that's my last goal here in life.

Death shall have to wait, the advocate said contentedly, and that's why I stay on my back in bed at night even though I cannot sleep. My dear lady, take my advice and never hurry. Don't get up to brush your teeth before the morning light, don't fret, accept the unavoidable, stay in bed at night, the trick is to sleep even when it's impossible. Who's got any teeth left to brush at my age anyway, Franjo added, although he'd seemed busy enough picking his own at the table in the Grotta Azzurra.

And then it struck me that today was a Monday, that the barber's shop in Buzet is closed on Mondays so that it must have been a coincidence that the barber was there when we passed, maybe only in order to tidy up, to sweep the hair off the floor, but that he could not have been expecting any customers, which made it especially insulting, turning up outside with his scissors at the ready, snipping away in the air behind the old advocate's back, an old, almost bald man, and to do this on a Monday, when the scissors are normally packed away, was an insult for which no other day of the week could have been used; and all this occurred to me while advocate Franjo was warning us against trying to find ways of avoiding the unavoidable, but I wasn't sure if he was talking about death or our modern times without communism.

That's my advice to you, my dear lady, the advocate said, but people in this town understand nothing and are running so scared that they now believe they'd better turn everything upside-down. Nothing must be done the old way anymore, each and every one of them is wriggling about like a worm on a hook, trying to get out of what's unavoidable anyway, twisting and turning, believing that it's all a matter of changing things and especially their own way of life. Surely you must have noticed this, my dear lady? How people in this country of ours persuade themselves that change itself will be a help, and I said yes, that's right, things are now very different from the old days, they imagine they'd be safe and given a roof over their head if only they'd change, the advocate said, and as for him there, the advocate said and pointed at my sweetie, he's no exception.

But my husband is not from here, I said.

But he's got this fixed idea that he must buy the empty house in Pelegrin, Franjo replied, even though his name is nothing like Bartolovic or Bartolo, in fact a name that has nothing at all to do with the house! In spite of not coming from here, he wants to buy the house in Pelegrin as if things in this part of the world suddenly would have changed. But we have no use for foreign names round here, the advocate said. Nothing here has really changed and least of all that house up there in Pelegrin, a house that has been there for more than two hundred years, staying the same all the time. It's the kind of house that never changes. It will remain as it is for all times to come. That's how a house of that kind survives change and interfering human beings, not the least bit concerned with us, a house that will keep standing there as it always has, regardless of us and our attempts to sneak away from our fate or, like him, and Franjo pointed again at my husband, trying to sneak into the house.

What do you know about the tunnel under it, my sweetie asked and now his voice sounded sharp, somehow wrong for such a hot day and quite unsuitable for addressing this frail old man.

I began to worry that his good mood might soon be over again, for his voice held no trace of the sympathy with which he had cared for the old man's legs and feet. The advocate had sunk back into his chair and seemed utterly exhausted. He was breathing with the greatest difficulty, his breaths came in bursts, and he had pulled a large white handkerchief out from a pocket in his vest, now wiping his forehead with it.

What tunnel, what silliness is this, he was muttering angrily, but without directing the words to my husband, and I could see that the advocate was totally exhausted and had no energy left for a real argument so soon after his lunch, even though he was the one who had started it, not my sweetie.

He took his time patting his forehead and bald pate, cleared his throat repeatedly and then began to examine his handkerchief as if he were alone with it in the room, as if only he and his handkerchief mattered and everything else was of no consequence, and for a moment I almost believed the handkerchief might have directed his mind away from us and all that had to do with the empty house; the old man seemed completely preoccupied by looking for something important in his handkerchief, forgetting that he was not alone in his office, now perhaps considering ideas or thoughts which I knew nothing about, but which I feared might distract him from our only reason for being there with him, the empty house on the other side of that wall in Pelegrin, *our* house, as my sweetie usually calls it. But then the advocate finally looked up from the handkerchief and from his stare, full of suspicion, I understood that he had forgotten nothing and that the handkerchief had nothing to do with what was on his mind, that he had used it simply to wipe his face, nothing else, and once it had served to mop his forehead and bald patch dry, he was quite ready to put it back in his vest pocket.

That house is not for you, he said. It doesn't suit you. Try to grasp this.

All we need is the owner's address, my husband said. We'll pay what it takes. We are just asking you for an address. Please, could you assist us in this matter?

The advocate looked up from his chair behind the desk and stared at my husband as if just that very minute he had stepped into the office. He looked him straight in the eye, but quite kindly, rather as if he was prepared to take an interest in this person for the first time this afternoon.

Do you get up before five o'clock in the morning, Franjo asked.

My husband looked baffled and stared back at the advocate.

No, he said.

Just what I thought, the advocate muttered and pulled out the large bottom drawer in the desk. From the drawer he took out a hotplate and put it on the desk next to the computer.

Do you know how many windows there are in the Pelegrin house, Franjo asked and my husband was unable to think of an answer and I stayed silent too, as I have never seen more of the house than what is visible from our side of the wall, not much more than the top of the gable facing us, a high, narrow gable, so how would I have been able to count the windows in the whole house?

Twelve, the advocate said in a loud voice, he now seemed to have recovered his strength. The house has twelve windows. But you didn't know that. And you didn't know that eight of them are on the front of the house. Nor that only four of the twelve windows are left for the rest of the house, for the back and the two gables. Of this you had no idea, the advocate said to my husband, but still you want to buy the whole house, windows included, he added, looking very pleased with himself.

This description of the empty house seemed to have brought back some of the old man's strength, as if thinking of the Pelegrin house had invigorated him and the listing of windows was only a start, but I was asking myself why Franjo knew so much about this particular house, given that Istria is full of houses, and even empty ones are not uncommon.

Eight windows facing directly east, Franjo said happily and went on to count each window on his fingers, not content until he got to the eighth on his right hand. It was as if, to his great satisfaction, he himself had taken over the entire house, *our* house, and now he moved on from its windows to the directions it faced. At this time of day the people living in the house would take their afternoon nap, Franjo said, contentedly looking at his watch, by now the sun is in the west at the back of the house, if you follow me, and up there with you in Pelegrin it must be almost as hot as down here with us in Buzet. And how many windows do you think there are on the back of the house? Its long western side, facing the cemetery? No idea? No idea at all, is that what you're telling me? Well, let me help you out, the advocate said and held up two fingers in front of his face, looking as if he wanted to have a cigar placed between them to round off the afternoon, a fat cigar, as there was more space between his fingers than he'd need for a cigarette, and the pack of Moravas that he had bought in the newspaper kiosk must have been put away in one of his suit-pockets, at least he had not been smoking since we left the Grotta Azzurra.

Two, the advocate said, keeping his two fingers splayed apart in front of him. The house never had more than two windows facing west. Eight on the eastern face, one on each gable wall, but only two on the whole west wall giving to the cemetery. And do you understand why? Because more windows would simply have made it too hot inside the house. Do you follow me? Too much sunshine, the advocate said and banged his fist on the desktop, just lightly, but still too hard for someone his age, for he started and I realized it must have hurt.

But I note that you're still up and about at this time of the day, Franjo said to my husband, but now in a subdued voice. You don't take naps and I guess you don't go to bed at sunset either, the way people used to in that house before we got electricity here in Istria. As soon as the sun went down the people who once lived in that house would go to bed. Do you understand what I'm telling you? They rose early in the mornings before it got too hot and went to bed early in the evenings because we human beings are meant to sleep when it's getting dark, even though I have reached an age when I cannot, the advocate said, placing his right hand on this chest as if this was where his sleeplessness was located.

In the past people slept properly at night and this didn't change until Italy brought us electricity so that it became possible to stay up in artificial light, even though it was dark outside and people should have been asleep, and for this I blame Mussolini, the advocate said. It was Mussolini and his electricity that ruined the whole idea of the house in Pelegrin, that idea being that people should rise with the sun and sleep at night, the same kind of thinking that two hundred years ago meant that having more than two windows facing west was totally out of the question. Now, do you understand? And all because of the heat, the advocate said. As far as possible the heat of the day must be prevented from getting into the house. They thought of everything as they planned and built that house some two hundred years ago, but all that was undone when Mussolini and his Italian electricity turned night into day, and the house was not built for such an unnatural extension of the day. Do you see what I mean? And that is why the house has been standing empty ever since, the advocate said, it's Mussolini's fault, his Italian electricity ruined many houses for us here in Istria, isn't that so, my dear lady, you know what I'm talking about, don't you? If it hadn't been for Mussolini these houses would not have been destroyed and the Italians who once lived in them wouldn't have felt that they'd do better by crossing to the other side of the border, leaving the houses behind since they couldn't take them along, empty houses ruined by electricity that had to stay here, making it necessary for a Bartolo to become a Bartolovic. That's how a man like Mussolini managed to lay waste a whole region, Franjo told my husband. And now you want to make it worse by moving into the house, to destroy it utterly, no doubt you've even got a flashlight, and your pockets full of batteries. That's how little you respect nature, said the advocate and looked straight at my husband. But you won't get the upper hand, that house is not for you. Try to get that into your head! It's just not for you. And don't put your faith in electricity! Our dear lady here can confirm what I tell you, the electricity here in Istria is not to be trusted, not in the least. It comes and goes depending on the weather, and your monthly bill is the only proof on a regular basis that it exists.

Only the house is trustworthy, the advocate said and felt in his pocket for the handkerchief. During the two hundred years it's been lived in, the house has been utterly reliable, built so that you sleep after sunset in cool rooms and get out of bed with the sunrise before the heat of the day takes over, early in the morning, before five o'clock, exactly as two hundred years ago, but here in my office and in the presence of witnesses you have confessed that you're not even awake at that hour, even though it's light outside.

What's that I've been confessing, my sweetie asked.

But during the day you're up and about, oh yes, though it wouldn't occur to you to go to bed when the sun sets, Franjo said reproachfully to my husband. But that's the kind of people the house is built for, not for someone like you, the advocate insisted, but for people who let the day be the day and the night be the night, who keep light and dark apart, for people who know what's theirs and what belongs to others, and by now the advocate was obviously pleased, in spite of making the house seem more and more uninhabitable with each new piece of information.

There can be no question of someone like you living in that house, he added, looking pleased as punch, as if the key to the house had now landed in his own pocket. What use would the house have for someone like you, Franjo said to my husband, who glanced at me helplessly; what on earth was he to make of a legal consultation like this?

He was visting this office for the very first time, and seeing this advocate only because I had urged him to. It was me who had brought him here, and now the advocate was wiping his forehead again with his handkerchief, then there's the view, he said to my husband, we shouldn't forget the view. What do you think about our countryside here in Istria? Have you taken the time for any sightseeing? Pretty countryside here, don't you agree? Especially viewed from the garden of the empty house in Pelegrin, a breathtaking view, and by now the advocate sounded rather like Dimitrij who spends all day watching his view, although on the other side of the village, looking at the Cicaria and the nature in Slovenia. From the garden of the empty house you can see half of Istria, all the way to Motovun, the advocate went on, and that might seem a good reason for wishing that the house faced towards the valley and not the east, so that from all eight windows now facing east you could admire the breathtaking southern view. Yes indeed! You might well have wanted to admire our celebrated Istrian landscape from each one of your windows. But the people who built that house weren't interested in your fine view.

Our Istrian countryside was of no interest to anyone two hundred years ago, the advocate said, his forehead shiny again, the sweat was dripping from both his ears, two hundred years ago our Istrian countryside was of no interest whatsoever although the very same landscape as today, in no way different, but wild nature was not worth discussing, much less admiring; a park, yes, that makes a difference, a park with neatly trimmed hedges and greenhouses and peacocks, now that would have been a different matter and much better than shapeless old landscape, and I am now talking of the people who built that house two hundred years ago, the advocate said, people who wanted the countryside out of sight at all costs, especially the countryside directly south of the house.

Directly south of the house, the advocate repeated. Now, do you see my point? Two hundred years ago the builder decided that the gable wall should have just one single window looking out over the valley facing directly southwards, in this way getting rid of both the sun and the landscape, Franjo said to my husband, so that the people who lived in the house wouldn't have to see all that useless countryside without shape, but above all to get rid of that sun out there, all that damn Istrian heat, Franjo said, and by now he was panting so heavily in between all his many words that I began to worry about him, walled in as he seemed by his own words. They wanted to keep the sun out at any cost, he went on, but I'm pretty sure you would have preferred to angle the long side of the house so that it would look out across the valley, just for the sake of the view and not understanding that with eight windows facing south the heat would fill up your house every day. Not even shutters would be of any use, the advocate said, the heat would be pouring into the house and soon drive you crazy, and that's why the house is not for you. You want to buy it, but you won't succeed. You understand nothing about a house like this. I advise you to buy another house, preferably in some place where people can pronounce your name. The world is full of houses, but the empty house in Pelegrin is not the right one for you, the advocate said, you don't suit it. After all, who are you? Here, in our part of the world? I'll tell you—nobody at all. And what do you imagine you'd become in such a house? Keep away from it, the advocate said to my husband. Now, that's my advice to you and you're getting it free of charge. A house like that is not for you. Our dear lady here ought to know, and look at her, she was content to buy the small house outside the wall, and at the time I was perfectly willing to act for her in my capacity as a lawyer, to help her with documentation and all the legal work, but your case is different. Completely different.

We had planned to buy it together, my husband and I, but in my name, I said.

It's no good, Franjo said. I see this case quite differently.

Again the advocate looked at his watch and suddenly he must have remembered why we were there, not because of the house, but because he had asked me to come along and pick up some papers from my insurance company, and he apologized.

I had almost forgotten about your documents, he said and pushed himself laboriously up from the chair with his hands on the armrests, and this time my husband did not help him. On slippered feet the advocate shuffled across the floor to the inner room, each of his two rooms were the size of a closet and separated only by a low threshold, and from the outer room we could watch him searching the shelves and desk in his inner room, the desk being just a small brown table without drawers, much smaller than the desk in his outer room, and while the advocate was looking for my papers next door he was mumbling to himself in Italian, *porca miseria*, mumbled the advocate, *sempre questi documenti perduti*.

But advocate Franjo seemed unable to find the right documents and the day was almost gone, the whole morning together with most of the afternoon had passed, and I could not help thinking about what the advocate had been saying about sleep and how the empty house in Pelegrin, *our* house, had been built for sleeping at night and during the midday heat; and I could not understand why he should take such a passionate interest in a house he could have no use for himself, a man who could not sleep, this house would only remind him of what he had lost forever, his good sleep at night and, so it seemed, also his afternoon nap. Why this interest in an old house, empty, forever with thick stone walls, that would do nothing but remind him of the big sleep awaiting him, the fact that he soon wouldn't be among us any longer, this fragile and almost transparent advocate with his wobbling head and now also with a bruised hand; a tender blue spot would soon form on his right hand which had struck the desktop hard in his outer room where we were sitting, and from the inner room I could hear him mumbling to himself, *non li trovare, non li posso trovare*, and then he came shuffling back from his inner room, empty-handed, without my insurance papers, to the outer room where my husband and I were waiting. *Non li posso trovare*, he mumbled, as if he had lost his way in his own office and now, already on our side of the threshold, he looked at us helplessly and said, I can't find them.

I can't find them, he repeated, but this time in Croatian, changing from the Italian he used in the inner room, as if the advocate were using a different language for each of his two rooms, as if Italian was used only for the inner room, not the outer, and then he sat down on the chair behind his desk again. There he sat motionless, and my husband said to me or maybe to the advocate, that it was time for us to leave.

You must forgive me, my dear lady, Franjo said and his voice was cracking. I simply cannot find your papers.

Never mind, I said. It doesn't really matter.

And we didn't get any coffee either, he sighed and looked at the hotplate on his desk. The coil of black flexible cord was held together by a rubber band.

Dear lady, do you take sugar?

It doesn't matter, I said.

Yes, yes, the advocate sighed. Motionless he was sitting in his chair, his eyes half closed again. Yes, yes.

I think we'd better leave now, I said. The advocate had closed both his eyes; he wasn't looking at either of us any longer.

But suddenly he looked up from his chair.

And how is your mother?

Thank you, I said. Mother is well.

Yes, yes, he sighed. Your mother back home in Fiume is well. Yes, yes. So she's feeling fine.

He nodded, and Fiume he must have brought back from his inner Italian room instead of Rijeka, for Fiume did not belong out here in the outer Croatian. But perhaps the advocate in his mind still was in the inner Italian room together with the papers he couldn't find although he now was sitting behind his desk in the outer Croatian room, but I didn't correct him; also my mother would not have objected to Fiume instead of Rijeka.

And the Colonel who died so young, the advocate said. He yawned. Such a handsome man, your father. Yes, yes.

My husband had got up, but Franjo wasn't looking at him, and I too stood up.

They were not so important, these papers, he said and now his eyes closed again, you can throw them in the wastepaper basket. But the papers had been left in the inner Italian room; here, in the outer Croatian one there were no papers for me to throw into the wastepaper basket. The voice of the advocate had sounded more faint than before, close to petering out; it looked as if he was about to fall asleep, his hands lying immobile in his lap. He was leaning his head my way without opening his eyes. Or had the large advocate's head, which he no longer could keep upright, merely slid sideways on his thin neck?

Could you please help me to loosen my tie, he asked and his voice was so thin and fractured that it sounded like an old-fashioned record, a scratched record played at too high a speed although his words followed each other slowly, barely carried by his voice, but so high-pitched that if the disc revolved just a little faster it would have been the voice of a *castrato*, not of a lawyer, and with such a voice it would not have been possible to win a single case in court, not with such a helpless, piping voice; and I bent down over Franjo, whose skin at close range looked almost transparently thin and faintly yellow under the pale surface, like old china but without its glossiness, and the carelessly knotted tie stuck out above the high neck of his vest and the knot looked worn and greasy, perhaps the advocate no longer knotted his tie every day, just pulling the tie over his head instead and tightening the knot like a noose, a single careless move and he could have strangled himself; and I used both hands to gently loosen his tie, but his eyes were still closed as if he now enjoyed being able to breathe more freely than before or had actually fallen asleep, and I didn't know if Franjo had a housekeeper or lived alone, all I knew for sure was that he had never married, but perhaps the advocate didn't even have anyone to clean or cook for him and his one hot meal each day was taken at the Grotta Azzurra, that dreadful place with its even more dreadful kitchen, advertising its pizzas in *Glas Istre*, burnt and sooty pizzas with a blob of half-melted cheese in the center of a lot of dough.

Perhaps this daily lunch at the Grotta Azzurra was all the advocate got to eat, and at first I thought of undoing also the top button on his white shirt, but there was no need, the collar left plenty of room round his neck, the thin neck the advocate hadn't had before, and the shirt-collar was edged with black and the inside wasn't clean either, thank you, Franjo whispered, you're both so kind to me.

He slumped in the chair behind his desk without moving at all, his eyes closed by lids almost without eye-lashes, and I was thinking that the happiest people are those who do not rebel against death, who are untroubled although death pursues them like a shadow all their lives, and how it is given to these happy people to die suddenly from strokes or heart attacks; people who fall over in the street and die instantly or in their sleep, so unexpectedly and suddenly that death doesn't get around to disturbing them, still fully preoccupied by living as they are, and now the advocate was really close to falling asleep, his head sagging on his chest.

A handsome man. Yes, yes. Died far too young, he whispered, his eyes had opened again and he was talking about my father.

Has your husband hurt himself?

The advocate's voice now was very weak.

It's only his hands, I said. He's cut them.

So he cut himself, the advocate whispered and his eyes closed again. Ah yes. Cut himself. Now, your husband is good to you, isn't he?

Yes, I answered.

He raised his head to nod, but then it sank back on to his chest again.

Tell him to take care of his hands, he whispered. Wounds suppurate. It's the heat, dear lady. Promise?

I promise.

Good, he said. You promise?

I promise.

Good. It's a promise.

My husband was standing near the door. Behind the advocate's back, he was pointing at his watch.

Please forgive me, the advocate said with closed eyes.

There's no need to apologize to us, I said and took a step towards the door, moving slowly as if I'd prefer to sneak out of the room, but truly because I did not want to disturb the old man and carry on the conversation as there was nothing more I had to tell him.

Close the door behind you please, the advocate whispered and it was high time to leave, my husband was looking cross and pointed to his watch again, and I bent once more over Franjo, who seemed asleep in his chair with his head resting on his chest, his chin covering the loosened knot on his tie. The advocate was breathing through his mouth and for a moment I was worried about leaving him like this, all alone in his office, but now my husband had already opened the door to the corridor outside. He'd had enough and wanted to leave.

What had we really achieved? And it was all my fault! I was the one who had explained how important and influential advocate Franjo is and how nothing could be done here in our town without his assistance, but now the advocate had fallen asleep. Disregarding his clients, he was sleeping in the armchair behind his desk and I had not even gotten my paperwork, these important documents he had persuaded me in the restaurant must be picked up from his office, but insurance documents that seemed to have lost their value somewhere between the inner Italian and the outer Croatian rooms in advocate Laginja's office, papers that had vanished, useless papers, however, as the advocate had assured me, and once again I bent again over Franjo and lightly stroked his big head as a goodbye.

My fingertips touched the bald, damp pate. The advocate slept. A sudden snore interrupted his quiet breathing, and I closed the door behind us.

It was already past four o'clock. In the streets of the town the dogs had disappeared and it is said that even the fish disappear in heat like this, that they flee into the cool, dark depths. Not even the fish can stand the afternoon heat without retreating down deep into to the sea, and in Buzet the fishmonger's slab on the corner was empty, stinking in the hot air, but we still ought to do some shopping now that we were actually down in Buzet. At home we had nothing, not even bread. We ought to go to Cico's or at least to the Albanian's vegetable stall; back home I had neither tomatoes nor cucumbers, not even any sweet peppers, but my husband said it was too hot for shopping.

Only the stones are on the move in such heat, all the stones buried in lawns and flower beds now work their way up to the surface of the cracked soil, dusty and gray, and my husband pointed at the roses planted in front of the Customs and Excise building, by now turned into a rose bed full of stones. Only stones cannot get enough of heat, and my husband explained how today's heat was the same old heat from yesterday, how the thunderstorm during the night had failed to shift it and how the old heat, like the dogs now, had simply withdrawn to some hidden place, staying away for some time, but ready to return as soon as the storm had passed, and the old heat was back again now, changing places with the dogs that had gone into hiding, just like the heat last night; and people round here call it "dog-heat," this heat that not even dogs can stand, a heavy greenhouse heat, dull and unpleasant to breathe, but with no humidity in it, and at home I didn't even have potatoes.

But my husband declared that he wasn't hungry.

Every time we should be shopping he says he isn't hungry. I'll fix myself a sandwich, he says. Yesterday's leftovers will be fine, he says, I have no appetite in the summer, anyway we eat too much, but towards the evening when he's got nothing special to do, he changes his mind. Then he forgets all about yesterday's leftovers and stands in front of the open fridge, inspecting the shelves, looking gloomy. Not even an egg, he'll moan. Where is my can of sardines? Only leftovers in here, and then he starts investigating whatever happens to be in the fridge. Where are my sardines from Vienna, he demands and produces something on a plate or wrapped in plastic that I've forgotten about and asks indignantly what's this, and I answer how should I know, already nervous because I know how this fridge-inspection will end; he won't eat any of the leftovers and I'll be accused of not keeping a properly organized fridge, everything is old, it's been here for days, he'll say, meaning whatever there is left on a plate or wrapped in plastic, inedible, my sweetiepie will say and hold his nose, and then he will scrape the stuff on the plate into the trash.

There's absolutely nothing here to eat, he complains. What kind of household is this anyway, who has stolen my sardine can from Vienna, he complains, and there is no use pointing out that he was the one who said he preferred eating leftovers and that we ought to have gone shopping in Buzet to get some vegetables at least, because there's not even an onion at home, and he'd be outraged if he found out that sometimes I even borrow potatoes from Dimitrij to make sure that my husband gets something other than leftovers to eat in the evening, if only potatoes from Dimitrij's vegetable plot below the empty house. If he only knew he'd throw one of his tantrums and shout that it's my fault that the fridge is empty, my fault that he's hungry and has nothing to eat and that someone has stolen his sardines from Vienna; and that's why I say nothing, and so he eats the potatoes on his plate in silence, not realizing that they come from Dimitrij. With Dimitrij or his wife he'll have nothing to do, and not with their potatoes either. I'm not even allowed to drink a cup of coffee in their place though everyone in the village is forever drinking coffee in each other's houses, but neither my husband nor I ever go to Dimitrij's, although it's Dimitrij who supplies him with potatoes, but without his knowledge. But coffee? My husband has forbidden me to have a cup of coffee with the neighbors, precisely because our neighbors happen to be Dimitrij and his wife.

If you allow Dimitrij and his wife to offer you coffee you will have to ask them over here, my husband says, who's always been keen on good manners. Form is much more important than content, he insists, and content without form is to him something inferior and detestable, however something typical of our Istria.

In this place both the people and the landscape are without form, just like in the rest of the Balkans, he argues, and almost everything he dislikes turns out to be lacking form: children who don't stand up in the presence of adults; people who put the knife into the mouth while eating; people who interrupt him or pick their teeth in his presence; who laugh straight in his face or stay silent, expecting to be entertained by others; or those putting on a gloomy look when they are bored, utterly unforgivable behavior according to my husband who is of the opinion that boredom mustn't show under any circumstances. It's everyone's duty to keep smiling even when there's nothing to smile at, but I am always trying to defend the children who don't stand up and the people who are bored without hiding it from my husband.

After all they are frank, I say, not hypocritical, but my husband answers that the frankness of strangers doesn't interest him in the slightest, that their views or thoughts are no concern of his and their feelings even less so. Life is unbearable if we pester each other with our private thoughts and feelings, he says, that's just the kind of sticky sincerity we don't need. The least one can ask is that people keep their mouths shut about what they think and feel, and telling about dreams is the worst kind of frankness to my husband, he cannot imagine any torment worse than having to listen to other people's dreams; that's what he keeps saying, my husband who refuses to dream out of principle.

Thank God we can impose form so that we can avoid pestering each other endlessly with so-called content, my sweetie tells me. Nothing but form distinguishes us from the animals and from those of our fellowmen who with their selfish frankness are not much different from animals, all these people ready to follow whatever notion comes into their heads, the kind of notions we would call instincts in animals, my sweetie insists, instinct being the only claim to so-called content that animals can make, but alas, most humans are little more than animals.

Too many of them are prisoners of their own so-called content and tyrannize the rest of us with it, he says, and there is no doubt that Dimitrij and especially his wife are that kind of people and that's why one shouldn't drink coffee with them or have anything to do with them whatsoever, under no circumstances except for emergencies, such as major church celebrations or an accident in the village, and a person who is all form and no content is always preferable to someone who is all content without form, a pleasing form already contains enough content, according to my husband, in this case form transforms itself into its own content, although most people, precisely because of their own formlessness, are unable to grasp this so that it never will occur to them that form provides more than enough content, and instead tend to believe that a very formal person must be devoid of content, totally empty, as it were, and in this my husband is right.

I know he's right as I'm one of these people he criticizes, convinced that my sweetiepie tries to save himself with the idea of form when he can't cope, but that his form is really insufficient although he calls it manners and a good upbringing, but unfortunately too rigid and brittle a form, threatening to push him back into hysteria and self-pity. But I don't dare say this to him and I don't stop my husband's carrying on with his exposition about the advantages of form at the expense of content and he does so, or at least he carries on as long as nothing more important attracts his attention, like just now, right now the heat's more important, it's far too hot to go shopping in Buzet, he said.

But I knew our fridge was quite empty, there was nothing edible at all in it, nothing that could be served up to fill my husband's stomach when he gets hungry in the evening, and on an empty stomach my sweetiepie becomes an utter misery, so quarrelsome no one can endure being around him, so I knew I'd have to borrow potatoes from Dimitrij again, from the very Dimitrij in whose house I am forbidden to drink even a cup of coffee, the man my husband does not greet and refuses to accept anything from as well as from his wife. That would be improper, and yesterday afternoon was the first time my husband forgot his own rules and principles, his enchantment with the empty house made him visit Dimitrij, but even so he had taken no coffee there, nor any of Dimitrij's grappa.

Once back in Pelegrin I parked near the church. There is no shade behind our house, but close to the church the great trees protect against the sun even during the hottest summer months, trees I don't know the name of, but which are in leaf the year-round. Throughout the year their crowns give shelter against sun and wind, three great canopies that have grown into a single mass of narrow, grayish-green leaves with downy, pale undersides.

All the way home I knew that my husband would go and see Beppo. I was convinced he would. The whole day was wasted and now we'd be back where we started. Our Monday had begun at Beppo's place in Pelegrin and now we were returning to Beppo and Pelegrin via the Land Surveyor's and advocate Laginja's office in Buzet, and during the entire drive back I thought of how my husband would speak to Beppo about the empty house, *our* house, as soon as we got home.

Beppo lives halfway between our house and the church, but at this time of day he would be sitting either next to the yellow mailbox in front of the church or on the stone bench just outside his own house. Beppo sat on the stone bench. It was already late in the afternoon and I knew it would be pointless to talk to him. Even at a distance his face glowed bright red and when we greeted him he opened his mouth, but couldn't close it again. His tongue was dark blue from all the red wine he'd been drinking and he had crossed his right leg with his left mostly, I think, to have a prop and prevent himself from falling over even though he was sitting down, not standing. It was already late in the afternoon and soon time for Beppo to go to sleep in the kitchen. But still he was there, sitting outside his house trying to eat cherries; most of them he seemed to have dropped on the ground, and behind his cracked glasses his muddy-looking eyes were staring out of the red face.

Did you enjoy my cakes, I asked.

What cakes, Beppo asked with his mouth full of cherries and I'm of course fond of him, his fate has moved me although he has never claimed or expected anything from me; for as long as I've owned my little house in Pelegrin Beppo has never done more than greet me good morning or good evening, never asked me for a favor, though year after year, every time I see him, I want to squeeze the swollen area round the bluish blackhead on his forehead and clear it out, then clean and dry the wound, even though I know it would be too much to ask. Never would he let me get that close, but still I cannot rid myself of this impulse, only do my best to hide it so that Beppo remains ignorant of my wish and all the other things I've thought of doing for him ever since I bought my house in Pelegrin, and I don't mean simply giving him one of my husband's pairs of cast-off trousers or bringing him a portion of hot goulash in the evening before he goes to bed, no, it's more than that, I'm talking about things that come straight from the heart and not out of a saucepan.

But I cannot tell Beppo any of all this, not out of shyness but because of sheer insufficiency, because my heart is too apathetic and weak. I'm not strong enough to show such care and I'm ashamed of myself when I see how Beppo is forced to live among us, wearing his torn, stained trousers and cracked glasses, with his unwashed neck and swollen hands with their broken skin; all this decay upsets me, even though I don't need to make it any of my business, but still it sometimes affects me so much that my heart aches for him. How much I wish that Beppo were clean and tidily dressed and could even feel a little happiness at times! But apparently he has no idea of what I would like to do for him and has never given the slightest hint by word or gesture that he understands my heartfelt wishes for him, which sometimes makes me wonder if he really deserves them.

Why do single men become so dingy, so entrapped in their own decay? Why should I notice Beppo's stains when he doesn't notice them or me? Or does he note the stains but just refuses to see me or anybody else? Does he prefer his cracks and his stains to being looked after? Is that why he has been living alone since his mother died, his ill, bedridden mother, fed and cared for by her son Beppo? His mother, who made and mended his clothes in her sickbed? But since her bed stands empty Beppo is alone and has no tasks. Now that his mother no longer stands in the way and he could lead a life of his own, it turns out that he has got nothing to fill a life with except what is no longer mended and patched, with nothing except this decay of his, and I would have liked to wash and mend his clothes and squeeze his blackhead, but Beppo would never let me, he would not allow himself to be helped. He does not need me and this hurts me, all this ingratitude makes me feel that he after all doesn't deserve the sacrifices I would be prepared to make to look after him, for *his* sake; and still, all I had once wanted was to step in as a mother for him the moment Beppo's real mother took to her bed.

She got a cold chill on her blood, or so they say in the village. The doctor from Buzet came and went, in and out of their house, but it didn't take long before he went away for good and left Beppo alone with his mother. He would turn her on her side at night and when her aches and pains made her throw herself out of bed he lifted her back, and during the day there still was more than enough to do, putting damp cloths on her forehead while his mother's frozen blood continued to work its way into her stomach and intestines; and the doctor from Buzet had long since given up visiting so that only Beppo, her son, stayed with her and had to do everything. Beppo held her on the bucket, emptied and scrubbed it, rinsed the bucket out with water from the garden hose and then brought it back in again. There was time for nothing else, and when one day the bed stood empty, Beppo too emptied and froze. Then he started drinking. Her blood froze solid and then her son's liver went on fire, or so they say in the village, and already on our way back from Buzet, long before we reached Pelegrin, my husband must have made up his mind to speak to Beppo about the empty house, there's got to be a key to the house somewhere, he said to Beppo, for sure there's got to be a key.

Every house has a key, my husband said. It's impossible to imagine a house without a key.

That is true, of course, and it worried me to think that he was right. Every house has a key, but my husband had no right to this one, just as he had no right to a house that wasn't his; it was bad enough that he had claimed the right to climb the wall, a deed he had paid for with his own blood. But Beppo remained seated on his bench, stuffing whole clusters of cherries into his mouth. Some of the stalks were sticking out of his mouth and his broken glasses were blinking as he peered at my husband, isn't that right, Beppo, my sweetiepie asked slowly, as if he was in no hurry and prepared to take his time, but still he had no right to speak to Beppo like that, I mean in that tone, and then suddenly my husband grabbed Beppo by his shirt-collar and pulled him up from the bench.

No, I cried, and the cherries fell out of Beppo's mouth as if he were trying to say something but no words came out, go and get that key, my husband shouted, the key, Beppo, get me that key now, stop it, I cried, don't you dare touch Beppo, but Beppo had understood and obeyed; on his unsteady legs he tottered back into the house and when he returned he was holding a large iron key with both his hands, the key to *our* house, and he gave it to my husband, who took the key and thanked him.

Thank you very much, Beppo, he said and bowed his head although not out of politeness, you'll soon get the key back, but after what had already happened I wanted no further part in this.

You mustn't, you have no right to the key and Beppo has no right to give it to you, I said, don't worry, my husband said, you mustn't humiliate him, I said, I want no part of this, but my husband couldn't be stopped, the empty house has bewitched him, he just smiled and said that I could go back home if I preferred.

Just go home and don't worry, he said. So I turned abruptly and left without saying goodbye to Beppo, disappointed with him as well, I'll soon be back, my husband called after me and I went home.

Why didn't I stay? To see a key in that lock! Why hadn't I forbidden him to unlock the empty house? But Beppo had given him the key and my husband's anger frightens me, his sudden, unpredictable fits of flaring rage without cause or direction so that I become their target only because I happen to be in the way. Still my husband claims that these outbursts come and go quickly, that they're over in no time at all, and this is meant to describe the nature of his rage, but even more as an apology. My anger has both a beginning and an end, my husband says, but because they lie so close together there is little space for what is there, all these stormy emotions not finding enough room; dense is what he calls his anger, and when there is not enough space it breaks out, his feelings suddenly overflow in all directions, feelings his surroundings would have been protected from if they only had stayed where they were meant to be.

But my anger is soon over, my husband always says. Like all passions my fury is quick to pass. In my case a fit of rage ends almost the same instant it overwhelms me, an outburst that goes away and leaves no trace, he insists, wanting me to accept that his raging is really a kind of internal cleansing; but what you do to sweep your mind clean I really don't understand, he says to me, meaning this more as reproach than amazement.

You crush all the emotions that upset you. It's like pressing plants for a herbarium, he says to me, you press them into something dry and crackling, parched mementoes of your own excellence, and he likes what he says, especially this "parched mementoes" makes him happy with himself.

You crush everything that has life and anything you cannot press into a form, my husband keeps saying, but don't forget that pressed plants leave traces too. Also a pressed flower discolors the finest paper, staining the pure, white surface with a dirty outline, and although my sweetie is speaking about sheets of paper and plant presses that don't exist, it is not clear to me why exactly his rage should have more form than whatever has been flattened in a plant press that doesn't really exist, well, this I cannot understand, only that what pleases him is that he has created a simile or a metaphor, an image of what is supposed to be my heart or my soul, and that his central idea has fixed on my capacity for staining his purity and myself too, by being so unemotional, always accepting and soothing and always prepared to forgive and forget, to restrain myself; and all this I can understand, I realize that what he says is close to the truth.

Still, he ought not to compare my emotions to plants. It is not for him to say, he who knows as little about plants as he does about animals, who never helps me in the garden and only needs a glimpse of Dimitij's Caesar outside on the path to the cemetery, to go straight back home and close the gate behind him.

After about half an hour, maybe a little longer, he was back. The bandages on his hands were dirty. He sat down at the kitchen table and asked me to get him a glass of water.

Where's the key, I asked him.

I've given it back, he replied.

Don't you ever hit Beppo again, I said.

My husband drank all the water in the glass and when he had emptied it, he made a face and said he hadn't hit Beppo, but that Beppo had lied to him, that everybody here in Istria is a liar. Dimitrij had lied to him and so had my lawyer. In this place every single soul bends the truth trying to work out how it can best be made to fit their own purposes and the truth that serves them best is the one that looks like a lie, my husband said, that suits them down to the ground, and after having dealt with Beppo, Dimitrij and Franjo in this way and called them all liars, I thought the moment had come to deal also with me, but my sweetie was silent.

I detest violence, I said. I cannot live with a man who hits people, but my husband only made a face again and said that it hadn't been the right key anyway. Beppo had given him the wrong key on purpose.

I climbed the wall, he said. But it was the wrong key. Beppo lied to me.

But he wasn't sober, I said, and yet I felt better now that it had turned out to be the wrong key so my husband had been unable to get into a house not belonging to him, that something had stopped Beppo from handing over the right key to the empty house, I guess all that wine he had drunk at Bruno's, or perhaps plain decency.

Don't you ever hit Beppo again, I said.

I didn't hit him, my sweetie said, yes, you did, I said, I didn't, he said, why should I hit him? I never hit him, my husband said, yes you did, I told him, I never did and never will, he said, sounding the way he does when he whistles Kálmán or Lehár; the way he whistles *Komm mit mir nach Varazdin,* the same thing over and over again in just the same monotone, though this time with a brutal ring and without any melody, perhaps because it was a lie and not a piece of music.

I don't want you to, I said, do you hear me?

But he was no longer listening to me. I'm so tired, he said, and reached out towards me, stretching both his arms across the tabletop and then bowed down until his head rested on it. I'm so tired, he said again, and I leaned over the table too and put my hands over his bandaged ones.

For quite some while we stayed sitting like that.

What are you doing there on the other side of the wall, I whispered. It frightens me. What is it you're searching for in there? I'm trying to understand, but everything I do makes you angry. All the time I'm afraid that you'll start yelling at me. Everything I do seems to be wrong, always, I said and sat up straight, but my husband didn't move, he did not even lift his head from the tabletop.

She's going to cry any minute now, he said without looking up, and I didn't know to whom he was speaking. That's the way it always ends. How many times have I asked her for one thing and one thing only? But my wife refuses to grasp that living together means adjusting to each other, that living together means to change. But not my wife. No. My wife says she has no intention of changing. Do I ever complain about what you do my wife asks, my husband said. No. The answer is no, of course she doesn't. But that's her way. My wife never complains, but only because she doesn't want to grant anyone else the right to complain about her, my husband said. No complaints, that's the reason why she keeps everything to herself. My wife stays silent for the sheer comfort of it, though she thinks of this as strength of character. At my age, says my wife, change is no longer possible, it's no longer possible to change one's character, that is what my wife says, my husband said, and it was me he was describing, and if anyone else demands anything from her she will say that she doesn't care and that it doesn't matter to her what other people believe or think about her, and by now he was not speaking to himself but to me, on the other side of the table.

Oh yes, now she's crying again, my husband said, and he was right for I was crying, you're like a child, he said, and once more I laid my hands over his and lightly stroked the soiled bandages, it seems blood and filth is all the empty house offers him, but my husband didn't move and didn't lift his head from the tabletop.

He was slumped forward over the kitchen table as if asleep. Sleep is always his last refuge. My husband escapes into sleep to block out the world. When he's asleep whatever threatens him in the present can no longer get at him and in this state it's impossible to bring him back to life, there he lies like a corpse, immobile until he wakes up strengthened and ready to take on the world again, but any kind of problem makes him sleepy and now he was breathing heavily as if he had really fallen asleep, as if the day had sapped his strength and what he had just said to me had extracted his very last ounce of energy; that was the sort of day it had been, but then he twisted his head sideways to speak, on purpose, he said, I'm sure he did it on purpose.

You mustn't say that about Beppo, I whispered. He looked after his mother.

Why do you always defend these people, he said and suddenly sat bolt upright. I'm the only one you don't care about.

Looking past him through the kitchen window I could see the empty house, but no more of it than what showed over the wall, its roof covered in tiles the same color as the house, and part of the flame-red facade giving on to the cemetery. Nothing more stuck up above the top of the garden wall, and after having spent a whole day preoccupied with the house and getting nowhere, at this distance it looked unreal to me; it was amazing to find it still there, just on the other side of our garden wall. Nothing but a high wall separating us from the empty house, from *our* house, nothing more than a wall of stone, and it surprised me that it was after all something so negligible, although high and topped with broken glass, but still nothing but a perfectly ordinary garden wall, and the shards of glass were glittering in the light of the setting sun, a big red sun now slipping out of sight beyond the cemetery, and I thought of what advocate Franjo had said about the many windows and the heat, and how the empty house was too large for just the two of us, too much of a responsibility for me, a house that I couldn't possibly manage on my own.

But how could I explain this to my husband? That what I'd hoped to own was never more than the little house, my own little house which had now become too cramped for him? How could I explain that what is not enough for him is just right for me, but still I tried and I asked him what would we have that big house for?

I want to give it to you, he said.

But all those rooms, I said. All those rooms and all the windows, ten of them.

Twelve, my husband said.

The house is just too big for me. I can't cope with a house that big.

Nonsense, he said.

I'm not so young any longer, I said, and I'm afraid the house is too big for us, but my husband didn't reply and by now the sun had almost disappeared below the horizon.

Nothing would really change in the large house, nothing that's important to the two of us anyway, I said, yes, it would, my sweetie said, there is nothing we could really change, I said, there is, he said, everything would be different. But that's what you said already when you moved in with me in the little house, you said everything would become quite different between us, I said to my husband, maybe I did, he said, but nothing happened, I said, there was no change, yes there was, he insisted, no

there wasn't, I said, none at all. That little house is different from the large one, my husband said to me, what do
you mean, I asked him, the big house is standing empty,
he said, we'll be starting from the beginning in a quite
empty house, he said, I don't dare believe that, I said,
we'll start all over again, my husband said, how could we,
I asked him but didn't dare say anything more, afraid
of saying something I would never be able to retract,
afraid that with one false word I would change everything I had said before into something different, in the
same way people can ruin their whole lives by a single
incautious act.

What do you know about the big house, I asked.

That it's standing empty and that there's space enough
for the two of us to start all over again, he said, again, I
said, again, my sweetie replied, surely there's nothing to
stop us from starting from the beginning again, and my
husband must actually have believed what he was saying;
after all the big house was standing there empty and although it wasn't his house he'd made it his in a way typical of him, and this is how he takes on even the most
hopeless enterprises, no walls or borders can stop him,
and I can't help but admire him for this, for his determi-
nation to hope and believe in what's on the other side of
walls, in spite of risking his hands getting bloody and
dirty in order to get there, but there's simply no wall too
high for my sweetiepie.

Have you ever deceived me, he suddenly asked.

He had turned his head away from me, and lying there like a lifeless thing across the kitchen table he seemed so far away from me that I reached out for his hands once more.

How can you ask me something like that, I said, knowing that this was no good answer to his question, but I couldn't reply to it, the way in which he'd put it, not just like that, and my sweetie was helping me out by not looking at me. Without realizing, he helped me and I received his help gratefully.

What are you doing over there on the other side, I whispered.

Nothing special.

That's not true, I said.

My husband sat up. He shrugged his shoulders.

That advocate of yours is a liar too, he said. There are three windows on the back wall. Not two. The third is almost overgrown with ivy. But it is there.

You don't love me any more, I said, but regretted it immediately. What had given me so much courage?

Do I actually mean anything to you, I asked, but my husband didn't answer, just waved my question aside with a gesture of his hand. The bandage was filthy, smeared with dirt, maybe he really was digging over there on the other side of the wall, my husband who's useless for any kind of work in our own kitchen garden, who can't tell arugala from a weed, and suddenly I became aware of how exhausted I was; I could no longer reach out to anyone, I felt close only to myself, my husband was only close to himself and to no one else, not to me any more, I who had wanted him so that I wouldn't have to be alone with myself.

I can see how lonely my sweetie is and for a short while in the kitchen we were together though separated by the table, although each of us was more alone than when we're off on our own, and at that very moment the phone rang in the other room. At the very moment of our being together in this silence that was ours alone, sharing each other's solitude, the phone rang and I rose from the table to answer it.

It was a woman's voice on the phone.

Pronto, who is this, the stranger's voice asked and at the same time my husband called from the kitchen asking who it was while I was listening to the stream of Italian words pouring out of the receiver, words that I had to sort out before I grasped that it was Signora Nina from Trieste who was speaking to me.

Si, Beppo had called her this morning from the telephone in Bruno's inn, poor Beppo who had to look after his mother all these years, Signora Fabris as it was, and Signora Nina's flow of words carried everything along, poor Beppo and the terrible heat wave, in Trieste it's so hot that nobody goes outside, the streets are empty, she said, and only after she had dealt with the weather did she get round to the empty house and what her husband might have to say about it all, because while it was true that they always agreed about everything of any importance, when it comes to men you can never be quite sure, Signora Nina said to me, and in order not to be drowned by all her words I kept saying *va bene* or *capsico* into the phone, who's phoning at this time in the evening, my sweetiepie was shouting from the kitchen, and he sounded the way he does when he quizzes me about Kálmán and Lehár, it was his irritated voice again, and I could hear that he had already forgotten all that had been said between us across the kitchen table, but Signora Nina's voice was pleasant and her stream of words was flowing down the line in one and the same direction and its course was approaching the empty house, *our* house on the other side of the wall; how thoughtful of *povero Beppo* to take note of our interest in their house, and Signora Nina had called us immediately after he'd been on the phone to her, but there had been no reply.

Perhaps we had not been in all day?

In spite of the heat we might still have been outside, up there with us, in Pelegrin, it's always cooler than down in Trieste where nobody now goes outside, that slight breeze from the valley makes the heat easier to bear up there in Pelegrin, much easier than here with us in Trieste, Signora Nina was saying in the receiver, it's the height above the sea, she explained, and only now had she at last got through on the line and been able to contact us.

So finally poor Beppo's effort had been successful and

it seemed to me that Signora Nina's flow of talk consisted as much of words she needed at the moment as of words she'd discarded at first, but then felt sorry for and therefore had decided to use as well, out of sheer consideration for all these useless words, and only when she had given me their address, *Piazza Peruggio numero tre*, did her store of words seem to be running out so that I could catch up with them and sort out what she'd been saying; but by now Signora Nina had finished, and I hung up.

Exhausted I went back to the kitchen and sat down at the table opposite my husband who was preoccupied with unwinding his bandages. Both his hands looked much better now. The wounds had almost healed and he said nothing, just looked questioningly at me with that dark look in his eyes which always makes me feel uncomfortable, for it bodes ill, a look I will probably never get used to.

Silently he unwound the bandages, taking care not to tear the scabs off the wounds; some had caught in the weave, but as my husband likes pointing out, he heals easily and meanwhile he kept staring at me until I said yes, they're prepared to sell. In fact they've always been prepared to sell and this coming Friday we're invited to their home in Trieste to discuss the deal.

Indeed, so they've always been prepared to sell, my husband said as he sat there at the kitchen table.

Both his hand were by now free of bandages and he

moved his fingers back and forth as if to convince himself that they were still there or to get them accustomed to no longer being under wraps.

So they've always been prepared to sell, he said. If someone is prepared to buy, that is. But there will be no buying and so no selling unless the price is right.

Signora Nina and Signor Antonio rented an apartment on the top floor of a building at a small square that seemed mainly used as a parking lot. Getting out of our car we spotted a lady dressed in unrelieved black on the highest balcony, pssst, my sweetiepie hissed, don't look, but I think that's Signora Nina standing up there.

Inside we walked up a dark, narrow flight of stairs, and their tiny apartment was furnished with dark, gloomy pieces of furniture, the kind that tend to be passed down within a family from one generation to the next. The Madonna with her child in her arms hung above the hall door and a little white dried seahorse and a shell on which someone had written *Ricordo di Napoli* were placed on top of the TV set in the sitting room, immediately to the right of the door to the balcony. From the other side of the square we could here church bells. It was Friday afternoon in Trieste. The church bells struck two o'clock, the shutters facing the square had been closed against the white sunlight and the heat, but in between the shutter slats the light filtered in, creating a pattern of stripes on the floor of the room.

Please sit down, Signora Nina said.

Her husband was seated in an armchair already. Both his hands were placed on the armrests, two fat and completely pale hands, and protruding from his white shirt was a solid head with greasy smooth hair as if Signora Nina's husband would have been ill with a fever, a completely colorless face except for Signor Antonio's nostrils, two tiny blue holes like a pair of ink spots on a blotting paper. All the features of his face crowded in close together and seemed so alarmingly vague and slight that they might disintegrate and vanish should you get too close to him and happen to breathe too hard on his face, and Signor Antonio stayed apart; he was sitting there alone in his own corner, seemingly not in the same world as the rest of us, sharing the table in the middle of the room at Signora Nina's request.

My husband is ill, Signora Nina said, as if an explanation was needed for Signor Antonio sitting there on his own, severely ill, but Signor Antonio raised his left hand from the armrest in a dismissive gesture as if he wanted to say something himself, but one could see that this was a gesture he had made many times before and he didn't complete it, his hand stopped halfway and somehow hung in the air for a moment before sinking down to the armrest again, there now, Signora Nina said turning to her guests, you can see for yourselves how seriously ill my husband is, it's nothing worth talking about, Signor Antonio said, please help yourselves, Signora Nina said.

On the table in front of us Signora Nina had already set out an open bottle of red wine, some ham together with a thinly sliced melon, cheese, a bowl of black olives and a small pile of white paper napkins, *sono i reni*, Signor Antonio said from his corner, my husband is very ill, Signora Nina repeated, what did he say, my sweetiepie asked, he's got something wrong with his kidneys, I translated for him.

His kidneys, my sweetie shouted, so loudly that Signora Nina turned her gaze in surprise from her own husband to stare at mine, at my husband who is also short of functioning kidneys or rather, actually has three, his own useless pair and a third, alien one that saved his life.

Dialysis, he shouted, turning to me, haven't I been telling you that I can spot a dialysis patient miles away, and he started speaking in the direction of Signor Antonio, explaining in detail the condition of his own kidneys, the diseased ones as well as the new, healthy one. Your body is just like a chest of drawers, my husband said to Signor Antonio, medical science nowadays can pull out a drawer just anywhere and put in a new organ and can you guess where my kidney went, I mean the one that doesn't belong to me, the healthy one, no, Signor Antonio said delightedly, looking as if he hoped my sweetiepie would tap his forehead and say "here," but instead my husband patted his belly, "in here," he said, and, indeed, it was quite true; the doctors had managed to fit in the donated kidney that saved my husband's life somewhere just to the right of his stomach, and Signor Antonio leaned forward from his armchair to examine my sweetie's belly, but I could see that it cost him a considerable effort and his forehead became damp with sweat, "in here," my husband repeated, and I hoped that he wouldn't unbutton his shirt to demonstrate the exact position of his new kidney, not in front of Signora Nina, this person unknown to us, someone I had only spoken to once before, on the telephone; that would have been improper, especially with the house in mind, I am almost sure it would not have made a good impression on her.

Nowadays none of our organs need to stay in the place nature found for them, my husband said. This is how it is with my kidney, I mean my third one that's strictly speaking not mine. Organs like that they just pop into any empty space they can find so that my kidney is where my appendix used to be before medical science got at it, my husband said to Signor Antonio, before the doctors just cut it out with their scalpels and threw it away on some dump for human refuse, and the place actually meant for an appendix instead became occupied by a kidney and, believe you me, I never missed that appendix, my husband cried while he kept patting himself on his right groin, never ever, my sweetie went on, although these days recycling is tremendously advanced which is true for modern medical science as well. And the bits and pieces we thought of as complete garbage in the past can be put to good use nowadays, that far at least we must give medical science its due, he said and Signor Antonio nodded gravely, *si, é vero,* he said and my husband, elated by so unexpectedly having found an attentive listener, started to explain all sorts of related things to him.

The only human progress you can really talk of is in the fields of medicine and crime, my husband declared, and what he had to say about different aspects of law breaking I think he had picked up while we were visiting advocate Laginja in Buzet.

Criminals and their methods are becoming ever more sophisticated and the same goes for medicine, my husband said, just think of how doctors today have found out how to surgically remove large pieces of skin from, say, the inside of the thigh, in order to stick the pieces on to accidentally damaged places after severe kinds of burns so that medical science no longer needs to use chicken skin, my husband said. And the advantage is certainly obvious, isn't it, I mean nobody would like to walk about with a face like a plucked chicken, wouldn't you agree, and Signor Antonio nodded in agreement, *non come un pollo,* he said and nodded again, hanging on to your own skin is clearly advantageous, anyone can grasp that, my sweetiepie said, while I to the best of my ability was trying to translate, but sometimes had to ask him wait for me to catch up, *é vero*, Signor Antonio said gravely, and while I was searching for the right Italian words Signor Antonio took the opportunity to ask about what the doctors actually do about the bare, skinless area, now left behind on the inside of the thigh; but my husband did not deal with that query in any detail, instead returning to the kidneys once more, and—delighted by their having so much illness in common—Signor Antonio also offered up his own kidneys, and so the two men quite forgot to serve themselves any of Signora Nina's ham and melon and cheese, and when they had dealt with their kidneys, so thoroughly that there was nothing more left to say about them, Signor Antonio and my sweetie started working their way through other internal organs, discussing the state of their livers and gallbladders or complaining about the way even the most expensive, up-to-date kidney medicines seem to interfere with other still perfectly functional innards, organs that are also of the greatest importance and in no way to be ranked below the kidneys, and all this I had to translate until Signora Nina turned to her husband and said Toni, I don't think our guests have come today to speak about your illness.

This was said in such a way that I understood that Signora Nina was in the habit of listening only to things she wanted to hear, and her husband immediately fell silent. Signor Antonio withdrew into his armchair, back into his own world where he had no need to raise his hand in order to get to say something, and it was a good thing that he was quite alone in his world, that there was no one there to listen to what perhaps was on his mind, because in the other world, the one where he didn't belong but in which his wife, my husband and I existed, Signor Antonio must long ago have had enough of being contradicted; or at least this is how he now looked, watching us with his tired, shiny eyes, and Signora Nina had noticed this also, how her husband had withdrawn into his own world, just as she probably hears and notices everything.

My husband takes his illness far too lightly, Signora Nina said. He's so thoughtless, she added, only sometimes, Signor Antonio said, and with his diet as well, Signora Nina said.

He forgets that he mustn't drink. Last year in Pisa the ambulance had to come and take him away, Signor Antonio's wife said, it was the weather in Pisa, her husband said. My husband is so thoughtless, Signora Nina said once more, and in his corner Signor Antonio was shaking his head, it was far too hot for me, Signor Antonio said, but no, at any cost you had to climb up the tower, Signora Nina said and her husband shook his head again, if it hadn't been so hot we'd never have needed to call the ambulance, he said.

What's the weather supposed to have to do with it, Signora Nina asked and sounded quite cross. My husband could have died in Pisa, she told us with her back turned to the corner where her husband was sitting, and by now we were all starting to eat the ham and cheese and olives, all of us except Signor Antonio, who had sunk back into his armchair again with both elbows placed on the armrests; his fingertips were meeting and supporting each other and the dim light in his corner made the nails on his short white fingers look as pale as his hands. But Signor Antonio didn't appear to be contemplating what had been said about his brush with death in Pisa, rather he seemed absentmindedly absorbed in awkwardly propping himself up, as if not only his body but his entire existence depended on his ten fingers alone, with nobody else around who could have helped him in any way.

My husband used to work for the Post Office, Signora Nina said, for almost thirty years, Signor Antonio pointed out, but his illness made it impossible for him to carry on, Signora Nina said. My husband's poor health meant that he had to be pensioned off although he was destined for something better, she said, well now, we know nothing about that, Signor Antonio said, his main interest in life has always been animals, his wife continued, not all of them of course, Signor Antonio said, but his illness cut all that short and if he weren't so ill we would never have sold the house, Signora Nina said, and this was the first time since we stepped inside their apartment at Piazza Perrugino *numero tre* that someone had mentioned the house in Pelegrin, *our* house as my sweetiepie calls it, and the way Signora Nina was talking about the house sounded as if she no longer considered it her own, but still not belonging to us.

RICHARD SWARTZ

My husband's kidneys got in the way, Signora Nina said, knocking her long black cigarette holder against the edge of the ashtray in front of her though it wasn't necessary; no ash fell off in the ashtray, the cigarette in her holder had gone out and Signora Nina didn't bother to light it again, though my sweetie immediately reached for the box of matches on the table, but instead of smoking she now balanced the black holder in her hand, making it look like a sixth finger, a totally black one and stiffer than the rest, and Signora Nina went on to say that when severe illness strikes everyone needs something to hang onto, or they'll just cling to their nearest and dearest so that not only the life of the ill person but the lives of an entire family could turn into utter misery, and in this respect her husband's position in the Post Office had been most helpful to him; all those pens and envelopes, the desk with the letter scales and rubber stamps, all those postal objects, each one of them in their proper place, had been most helpful to her husband as well as all the considerations shown by his superiors, and of course also his specialized knowledge about how to receive a telegram by telephone, knowing that Ancona stands for the letter A, Bari for B and so on and so forth.

In this way her husband's Post Office employment had provided much to hold on to, not least the fact that his already diseased kidneys had profited from this work. Her husband's kidney tests had never been better than during those Post Office days, Signora Nina told us, and with this fact in mind and with the benefit of hindsight it must be admitted that it had been a mistake to give up such a post because of ill health, given that this excellent post certainly had been helping to hold back rather than worsening the disease. It was only when my husband left the Post Office that he became seriously ill, Signora Nina insisted, and in his corner her husband was nodding, è vero, Signor Antonio said solemnly; indeed, only after giving up the work at the Post Office had his kidney tests gotten really worrying and more acute crises occurred than ever before, and no one could have imagined anything like that during the time he still went to work every day, although already ill.

Isn't that right, Toni, Signora Nina asked, si, he said, but what happened in Pisa was due to the weather, but by then his wife had finished with Pisa and just repeated what she'd already said: that it was when her husband left his Post Office job in order to look after his health that he really fell ill.

The Post Office helped my husband to think of other things besides his illness, Signora Nina said, and the fact that the window where he served could be closed at will had a beneficial influence too. All these customers with their complaints, always wanting to state them straight away! But fortunately there was the window, my husband could close that window of his at any point in time when a customer was getting too demanding, Signora Nina said, thank goodness for such a window! Time and again people, upset about something, insisted on presenting their complaints directly to her husband in spite of the posted regulations stating quite clearly that all complaints should be made by registered mail to the special authority for Post & Telegraphy in Rome, to all extents and purposes just like a real Ministry, and not to the local Trieste office, and sometimes my husband would close the window for no particular reason at all, Signora Nina said. Doing that could be a real boon to his kidneys and such a break didn't add much to the customers' wait. Surely a short break is not too much to ask when your health is at stake?

And besides, his position had meant such a lot to her husband because one of his colleagues had been very supportive, someone he could confide in, isn't that right Toni, Signora Nina asked and turned towards the corner where her husband was sitting, *si, è vero,* Signor Antonio said, he was my husband's best friend at the time when he was still reasonably healthy, Signora Nina said, Signor Tartini, Signor Luigi Tartini—and they both came out with the name almost simultaneously so that you might have thought that Signor Tartini was as much a friend of Signora Nina as of her husband—a very caring colleague who recognized at once my husband's artistic talent, Signora Nina said, and Signor Antonio nodded.

My husband was writing quite a lot at the time, she went on and Signor Antonio's right hand moved slightly, as if emphasizing that although there was some truth in what his wife was saying, not that much had really been written, and Signora Nina noticed his objection as she probably sees and hears everything, but went on regardless.

A fine handwriting like my husband's could have taken him into a career quite different from what fate and his kidneys determined for him, she said. You two have met my Toni only now but believe me, he's only a shadow of his former self. Well you can see for yourselves, can't you, Signora Nina said, but in other circumstances all kinds of doors might open to someone with such a handwriting, although it's hard to imagine now.

You can see for yourselves, Signora Nina repeated and glanced towards the corner where her husband was sitting in his armchair, but without seeming at all irritated he waved this comment away with his right hand, a hand which looked like a white handkerchief waving in the dim light of his part of the room.

Such a handwriting has always been in great demand in the ministries in Rome, and also here in Trieste it could really have taken him places, Signora Nina insisted. And my husband even wrote poems! Once he brought a poem instead of flowers for my mother on her birthday on November seventeenth, it was in nineteen fifty-three, she said, for Mother's birthday, Signor Antonio said, and my mother always agreed with me, Signora Nina said, handwriting like my Toni's was something one didn't often come across, this side of the war. And she liked the poem too, remember Toni?

So you write poetry as well, now that's interesting, my husband said, turning towards Signor Antonio's dark corner of the room.

But Signora Nina's husband didn't answer and nothing moved in the shady corner, until instead of a reply a pale hand looking like a handkerchief fluttered once, and Signora Nina went on to tell us that from the very start Signor Tartini had encouraged her husband to write, Signor Tartini who himself wrote poetry in his leisure time, and in this way too was a good influence on her husband, but in his thoughts her husband was still constantly preoccupied with his illness, and so made it worse. Without his Post Office position he had too much time on his hands, time that became occupied by the illness which had now taken over and settled down in all this abundance of time, and made itself at home as it were, and because her husband hadn't made use of all of it he had allowed the illness to do it, Signora Nina said, such a fatal mistake, and in this Signor Tartini agreed entirely with her, isn't that so Toni, she said, but her husband didn't answer, such a concerned colleague and so very talented, Signora Nina said, my Toni could have learnt a lot from him if he'd had the mind to, *si*, Signor Antonio said gravely, also in areas other than just the postal matters, she said and her husband did not contradict her, on this issue they were in agreement.

Tartini wrote poetry, you know, Signor Antonio said from his corner, I've said that already, his wife said, beautiful poems, he said, with rhymes, Signora Nina said, without rhymes as well, her husband said, but Signor Tartini's poetry was of course more artistic than my Toni's, Signora Nina said and her husband didn't contradict her, he had stopped speaking about his own and Mr.

Tartini's poetry, but you disappointed him, Signora Nina said to her husband. You had more time for your illness than for your friend, but Signor Antonio still made no comment, just sat there quietly in his corner observing us, his wife and the two guests who were visiting him for the sake of an empty house.

Signor Tartini regularly sent poems to *Il Piccolo* that he had written himself, Signora Nina said, but her husband made a somewhat dismissive gesture, maybe not regularly, but anyway, her husband said, the papers then were quite different from nowadays, Signora Nina said.

In those days they took the trouble to publish also nice news once in a while, things for people to enjoy when they'd had enough of illnesses and other problems at home. Of course it's true that although the war was over by then you could still find more than enough unpleasant matters even in a paper like *Il Piccolo*, Signora Nina said, but one could always turn the page over and suddenly, right there in the middle of the next page, one could find a piece of nice news or a nice poem by Signor Tartini.

Remember, Toni? Mother and I would always look out for his poems, because what he wrote was very nice to read, although not always true. Art is like that, Signora Nina said. Much of it is just made up. But what a newspaper prints must of course be true, I mean when it is not a poem. That's why reading the papers is so disagreeable these days, Signora Nina said, and for a while now Signor Antonio had been moving about anxiously in his armchair, as if he wanted to protest some of the things his wife had been explaining to us, but this time she didn't notice what was happening in his corner and besides was now taking place behind her back; and Signora Nina hadn't finished with the newspapers yet, things that aren't true shouldn't be allowed to be written at all, she said, but every day the newspapers are full of lies as if these days there's no difference between one's daily paper and a poetry book.

You should just hear what my husband has to say when he reads his daily paper, Signora Nina said, and again Signor Antonio tried to object, but rather quietly and without conviction, a mute protest, as if he didn't want to make too much of it, isn't that so, Signora Nina asked and turned round in her chair, surely you can't deny that you're irritated by all these lies they put in the papers every day? Yes, also Signor Tartini used to be terribly irritated even though the columns of *Il Piccolo* were always open for him, but . . . but, Signor Antonio protested, and for the first time I heard him stammer, but maybe just because he was upset, and it must have been his wife that upset him with her talk about art and the newspapers, or perhaps it was that phrase about *Il Piccolo*'s open columns that he was objecting to, although his agitation might well have been caused already by her descriptions of his routines at work; after all, it was Signor Antonio who had worked for the Post Office, not his wife.

If there was an authority on postal matters in the

room it was not Signora Nina, but her husband, and while she had been laying down the law about the world of newspapers and how it treats the truth, my sweetie too had started twisting in his chair with frustration. Obviously he had forgotten about the ham and melon still on the plate in front of him and I could see that he too wanted to protest something, just like Signor Antonio, but was even more inhibited than our host who at least could argue with his wife in her own language while my sweetie had to rely on me, trust me to take his point of view and do justice to it, translating for him, which is something that fills him with disbelief every time, convinced as he is that I shorten and distort what he says, that I interpret rather than translate, and that my interpretations reflect my inability to truly grasp what he means, rooted in my unwillingness to even try to render properly what he wants to say in another language than his own; and all this upsets him.

I'm completely at your mercy, my sweetie keeps saying, he doesn't realize that each language defends itself against experiences made in another one, I am subject to your every whim he says, and since he understands some Italian, although much less than he's willing to admit, he has ideas about what people are saying before I translate for him. He tells me that I shorten and distort, that I fail to translate exactly what he says or what someone says to him, and that this, my lack of sensitivity leads, or so my sweetie thinks, to the most devastating misunderstandings; and according to my husband this habit of mine of interpreting rather than translating is typical of me and my way of coping with the world around me, that it is in my nature to have no interest whatsoever in being as faithful as possible, to do justice to the world around me, but instead giving way to the kind of vague imprecision which conclusively proves, as far as my sweetie is concerned, that women are slaves to their emotions, just as no woman can ever learn how to cook according to a written recipe, preferring to let her feelings guide her, and rather than following instructions fries in pans that are too hot, boils things for too long, adds too much salt or too little; and whatever I leave out or shorten when I'm translating is my way of exerting power, my typically feminine way to exploit his lack of spoken Italian, his pretty total lack in fact, barely enough to allow him to believe that I don't pay him the compliment of trying to render as precisely as possible what he has said or what someone has said to him, and in this I share the carelessness and flippancy which characterize most women and disturb all attempts at the logical ordering of—in this case—the beautiful Italian language, not to speak of his own arguments and those of the person who's been trying to talk to him, in Italian as it happens: my inexactitude and impatience also constantly cause disorder in his own thoughts and perceptions; and it is I, his own wife, who allegedly is responsible for such disorder, nobody else than me and my way of treating the Italian language.

But while the two men present in the room were by now anxious to show that they objected to the incomplete and imprecise things that Signora Nina had been saying in her feminine way, she carried on with her description of the differences between a newspaper and a book and between truths and lies, or if not sheer lies at least something made up by imagination, we should never mix up a book with a newspaper, Signora Nina said while my husband and Signor Antonio were wriggling, both of them looking ready to protest at any moment, everything that's made up just makes us nervous, Signor Antonio's wife said.

Now, if the paper tells us that there's a war on between two African states, well, then it had better be the case, Signora Nina said. Then there should be a real African war going on while in a book it's perfectly alright to start up a war just anytime although there is no such thing happening in real life. A war in a book can be completely made up and it doesn't matter at all, it's even possible to invent book-wars that in real life would be unimaginable, Signora Nina said, one can find books with wars that have turned the whole world into a wasteland and yet not one person alive on earth has been hurt in the slightest. The world is still there, whatever the book says. But such a war has nothing to do as long as it doesn't exist in real life in a newspaper. That's the way it has to be in a newspaper, while the entire population of China might be killed off in a book if necessary, just a page or two would be enough, though of course your papers are not like ours, Signora Nina said, now having turned to me, as a person from the other side of the border.

Your newspapers still never publish the truth about the war and what happened then to us Italians, and if your papers print any figures they're either too large or too small. All our Italian numbers are too small and your Yugoslav numbers too large, *si, i grandi numeri,* Signor Antonio said, and all this in order to take over our land and our houses for good, isn't that so, Toni, Signora Nina said, *assolutamente,* Signor Antonio said. You don't want to hand our houses back because you like to believe you won the war, Signora Nina said. But your newspapers never contained one true word about the war, those papers that used to have that hammer-and-knife thing at the top of the front page, so that it was clear at once what kind of paper it was, Signora Nina said and Signor Antonio nodded agreement, even before opening such a paper you knew straightaway that it would be full of incorrect figures and lies, page up and page down, nothing but lies, her husband said from his corner, your newspapers didn't even get the weather right, Signora Nina said, they even lied about the weather, Signor Antonio said, that's right, his wife said, and when we all fled across the border to Trieste after the war, we left Istria because we were sure nothing good would come of numbers like that, never tallying with our Italian ones.

That's how your newspapers used to be in those days, Signora Nina said, a war is never a good thing, Signor Antonio said.

But I'm told that these days you have books with the proper figures, Signora Nina said to me, but I still don't read them. Why should I? I know the right and wrong figures anyway. I was there after all, Signora Nina said, so why should my husband and I bother with reading in your newspapers and books about what we've been part of ourselves, don't you agree with me, Toni, a complete waste of time, Signor Antonio said, my husband is quite right, Signora Nina said, we know what it was like and we don't need your books, and by now she must have felt that the moment had come to start smoking again and put the holder with the extinguished cigarette to her lips, Signor Tartini too was of the same opinion, Signora Nina said. Signor Tartini also regarded the whole of Istria as Italian.

The black holder with the extinguished cigarette looked quite splendid against her red lips. Signora Nina leaned across the table towards my husband, but only a little, as if she was not really in need of his assistance, but still he at once reached for the box of matches on the table, struck a match and lit her cigarette. Signora Nina was now smoking again. She blew the smoke across the table and looked about her challengingly, but since she seemed in no mood to put up with any objections, and only required agreement, both my sweetiepie and I stayed silent; also Signor Antonio in his corner had nothing to add.

I think we were all feeling the heat and in that regard Signora Nina hadn't been exaggerating—the heat in Trieste is much worse than up in Pelegrin, being so high above sea level does help to make these July days more bearable. But I would have thought that having the sea so near would help to cool the air in Trieste, the Adriatic sea that was not more than a few blocks away from us, though hidden from sight by houses and walls. In front of the city the colorless and quite still sea was lying out there in the bay, a smooth shiny surface reflecting the city of Trieste, a merciless mirror of stagnant water, and from this mirror the heat was sent into the streets of the city and even up into this apartment, several blocks away from the harbor and without a view over the sea, and the little white seahorse and the shell from Naples on top of the TV set, so far away from Molo Audace and Canale Grande, seemed even more exposed to the heat, out of their element as they were. The heat was filling these rooms at the very top of a building where the walls could not keep it outside, the tiles and tin on the roof didn't give the slightest protection, but instead turned this Trieste apartment into a trap; there we were, imprisoned by the heat, closing in on us from all sides, and without the breeze that softens even the worst day back home in our Pelegrin.

Such a beautiful name, my sweetiepie said, and this name he could pronounce on his own without translation, Luigi Tartini, and he had now turned to Signor Antonio.

Signora Nina was still occupied with smoking the cigarette my husband so attentively had lit for her, my husband who is often complimented on all these little chivalrous gestures of his although I'm the one who usually gets to hear the praise, which seems always offered up without the currently charmed person realizing that my husband is more calculating than genuine, that in fact there is more cunning than care behind his nice manners, and his decision to mention how attractive he found that name, Luigi Tartini, rather told me that he hoped to use it to get round to our only reason for spending the afternoon in Trieste, the empty house in Pelegrin, and it was only because of wanting to buy the house that he turned to Signor Antonio who was showing so unmistakably that he held a different opinion from his wife as she was holding forth on newspapers, the art of poetry and her husband's illness, even if he hadn't been able to say so at the time.

I had the impression that my husband hoped to forge a link with Signor Antonio which might be to our advantage in settling the matter of the house, *our* house, and help bring to a close the negotiations that hadn't yet started, although the church bells had chimed once more outside, it must by then have been after four o'clock in the afternoon; or, at least, this was how I understood my husband's move although I didn't see how he could imagine that Signor Antonio might be made to side with us against Signora Nina, his own wife, and still less what Signor Tartini had to do with the house in Pelegrin, how much poetry there is in a name like his, my sweetiepie said to Signor Antonio, and I translated what he had said.

You really find it pleasing, Signor Antonio asked, and you could hear from his tone of voice that he took satisfaction in how perceptive my husband was, that there

RICHARD SWARTZ

was something especially poetic about the name Tartini, you must have been very close friends, my husband said, but at this point Signor Antonio's wife joined the conversation.

My husband ruined that friendship with his illness, Signora Nina said, and by now she too had turned round in her chair; the conversation had left the table in the middle of the room where she had been in charge and shifted to the corner where her husband was sitting alone instead, and it was my sweetie who had managed this change of direction, forcing Signor Antonio's wife to turn around in order to keep an eye also on her husband.

Signor Tartini was a model for my husband, Signora Nina said. A model more than a friend. We can't call it true friendship, not in this case. I don't know about that, Signor Antonio said, you don't know, his wife said sharply and stared at him, yes, Tartini was a model, of course, Signor Antonio said, there now, you hear what he's saying, Signora Nina said to us, but he meant more than that to me, her husband went on. I was very fond of him.

Perhaps your wife is trying to say that at times such admiration might stand in the way of true friendship, my sweetie said, a beautiful thing, isn't it, Signor Antonio sighed. Friendship, I mean.

He encouraged you, Signora Nina said snappily. But then you fell ill.

Yes, he encouraged me, her husband said, I've already said that, Signora Nina said.

I showed him some of my poems, Signor Antonio said, like the poem for Mother on her birthday, Signora Nina reminded us.

Yes, the birthday verse.

And others as well, Signora Nina said.

Yes. I plucked up my courage.

And then this competition came along, Signora Nina said, turning to us and putting her cigarette holder with the glowing cigarette in the ashtray.

A competition announced in the newspaper, Signor Antonio said, it suited my husband perfectly, Signora Nina said, yes, her husband said, it suited me perfectly, I've said that already, his wife said. It was a competition about animals.

Yes, Signor Antonio said. The topic was "An Animal Worthy of Our Admiration."

That was the theme of the competition, Signora Nina said. The person who wrote the best entry about an admirable animal would win the first prize. It was a competition that seemed made for my husband, he's tremendously interested in all kinds of animals, she said, not all them of course, Signor Antonio said, but his wife went on to tell us how from the very beginning her husband had wanted to write about the horse, no other animal means as much to my husband as the horse even though he has never gone riding, not even when he was perfectly well, Signora Nina said. My husband always liked horses although he kept out of their way. He just admired them from a distance, but he had no wish to write about any other animal and certainly not about a dangerous one, Signora Nina said. What interests my husband are domesticated animals and to him the horse was the ideal domestic animal, even though in the beginning he had been considering the dog. Naturally it would have been a great help if we'd had a dog of our own so that my husband could have studied it at close range, Signora Nina said, I always fancied having a boxer, Signor Antonio began, but his wife immediately interrupted him, people with kidney failure cannot have dogs.

If a member of the family suffers from kidney disease a dog poses serious risks of infection, Signora Nina insisted and my husband agreed with her at once, a dog is totally out of the question in a home where someone has a kidney problem, he said and Signor Antonio hurriedly joined the consensus, *certo*, a dog would be an impossibility, that's how my husband's studies of the dog came to nothing, Signora Nina said, my husband was already ill enough, his kidneys were practically making him blind at the time, isn't that right Toni, Signora Nina asked her husband, *è vero,* Signor Antonio said, and then a dog on top of all this, Signora Nina exclaimed, how thoughtless!

So my husband began writing about the horse instead, Signora Nina went on, but first he had to study what had already been written about this creature, *La cavallina storna*, Signor Antonio said, turning to my sweetie, you may have heard about this work before, and to my astonishment my husband said that he had, *si, naturalmente,* he said, then you'll understand how I felt, exclaimed Signor

Antonio. What a mistake! To even think of competing with Pascoli!

As if Tartini hadn't been challenge enough.

Signor Antonio sighed, looking not only ill but quite depressed at the thought of how, at the time, his own horse might have been judged by the standards of both Pascoli and Tartini. To compete with such a famous horse and the skills of his writing rivals—Signor Antonio decided that carrying on with horses would have been bad for his health and added that besides, it would have been a mistake to write about the horse in general, instead of sticking to just a single one, any one horse.

Imagine how I felt, he sighed, my husband just will not listen to good advice, Signora Nina said, descriptions of horses and books about them fill whole libraries, Signor Antonio was explaining to us, there are so many of them. Any further attempt to write on the subject has to add something new to what we already know about this admirable animal, something that might not have been known before, something still missing and therefore necessary to complete the subject so that, after such an essay, it should be . . . how can I put it, Signor Antonio asked, exhausted, my husband said, yes, exhausted, that's the word, Signor Antonio said, looking gratefully at my husband.

Afterwards there'd be nothing more to say about the horse, Signor Antonio concluded, that is to say of the horse as a natural phenomenon, and my mistake was fancying myself the right person to write it, that article about the horse for the animal competition in *Il Piccolo*, his wife said, *si*, Signor Antonio said, there was a time when I believed I was the one to do it.

Maybe you were, Signora Nina said.

No, her husband said, we'll never know, will we, Signora Nina said, yes we do, Signor Antonio insisted with unexpected firmness from his corner of the room. We know all right, and we know even more than that, and his wife fell silent.

These words were spoken with such authority that for a short while Signor Antonio seemed more tangible than before, as if suddenly equipped with a new, sharper outline, but then he sank back into his armchair again, and his wife told us that the kind of exhaustive horse-description that her husband had struggled to compose had seemed pointless to her already at the time; as for herself, she'd never dream of reading anything like that, at most maybe something about how beautiful this animal is, also with a rider astride its back, or something about the well-known faithfulness of horses, and this must have been what Signor Tartini had in mind when her husband didn't finish writing about the horse, because Signor Tartini had pointed out that her husband would have had a better chance to win the "An Animal Worthy of Our Admiration" competition if he perhaps tried to limit his subject matter rather than studying books full of nothing but horses; after all, a newspaper like *Il Piccolo* isn't there to print a whole thesis, Signora Nina said.

But this kind of attitude is so characteristic of her husband and was so long before his kidneys were attacked by the disease, this tendency to either limit the goals he set himself in life, thus trying to ensure that he would actually achieve at least a few of them, but failing to understand how his own caution tended to make them quite minor, even pointless, or—and this Signora Nina felt was even worse—her husband's tendency to be unable to impose any limits at all on his life-goals, goals which as a result became unattainable, staying forever out of reach; and that horse, Signora Nina told us, was an example of the latter.

Signor Tartini had realized this too, Signora Nina said. From the very beginning he was against the horse. Instead Signor Tartini had suggested a different animal altogether, a smaller one, but now her husband was shaking his head.

Tartini had no views on the animal's size, he said. To him the only thing of importance was how the story of the animal was told, Signor Antonio said, what nonsense, his wife said. Any animal was good enough for him, Signor Antonio said, Signor Tartini did not want you to have anything to do with the horse, his wife insisted.

Why didn't you write about cats, my husband asked.

Cats, Signor Antonio said, sounding surprised.

Yes. They're smaller than horses but still a kind of domestic animal. Why not cats?

The wrinkles deepened on Signor Antonio's forehead, damping with sweat. The room felt airless. Signor Antonio stared up towards the ceiling, looking as if an entirely strange animal had been mentioned and he now had to try to imagine what it might be before he could consider its use to him.

No, he said after a moment's silence. I couldn't have written about the cat.

Just a thought, my husband said, but I was struck by the idea too; I for one found it hard to imagine Signor Antonio on horseback, but had no problem picturing him in my mind with a cat on his lap. Sitting there leaning back into his armchair with the faded glow of the lamp falling over him, the animal that Signor Antonio had so brusquely rejected would have been the most fitting: a cat, whose body, curling tail and slanting, sleepy eyes, would almost have merged with the shapeless pallor of his own, *impossibile*, Signor Antonio said, *assolutamente impossibile*, and it was the cat he meant.

But in the end Signor Tartini had managed to persuade his colleague to concentrate on an animal other than the horse, it was Signor Tartini who got my husband to change his mind and take on a less prominent animal, Signora Nina said, and Signor Antonio explained that in the end he had come to realize that the papers he had already filled with notes on the horse would add nothing new to what was already generally known about this particular animal and, still worse, that his own experience with regard to horses was much too limited to make up a complete horse, at least not one fit to be presented in writing.

Tartini himself was of the same opinion, Signor Antonio said, there you are, you admit it yourself, his wife said.

So the option of choosing a smaller animal was discussed and also in this respect Signor Tartini had behaved like the true friend he was. Look here, he had said one day in the Post Office, pulling a small book out of his pocket, we had just closed our windows to go and buy cold meat for lunch at Prodan's deli on the corner, Signor Antonio explained, you never told me that, his wife said crossly, you know that the doctor told you to be careful with your diet; and it must have been the delicatessen that annoyed her, as if the delicatessen together with her husband's thoughtlessness would have been responsible for his serious illness, the fact that his kidneys needed to be helped along by a machine every third day.

But her husband had lost all interest in both the dialysis machine and the delicatessen, he wanted to speak now about the book that Signor Tartini had lent him, a small, slim book with a yellow cover, which Signor Tartini intended as an inspiration for his colleague to help him pick another competition animal, quite different from a horse, a little animal book from Signor Tartini's own bookshelf.

That's the kind of friend I had in Tartini, Signor Antonio said, far more than just a model, and he had put the book in his pocket and not looked at it until the Post Office work was over for the day and he was back home, remember, Signor Antonio asked his wife. It was a Friday, just like today. I had the whole weekend ahead, plenty of time to read, he said, and to this Signora Nina had nothing to add, and as soon as Signor Antonio had opened the book and started reading, he had realized what his friend had meant by inspiration.

In the book a human being is turned into an animal, Signor Antonio said, there now, you can hear for yourselves how disgusting, Signora Nina said, making a face as if the book had been an insult to her already at that time and it now annoyed her that it was even being mentioned again.

All made up, anyone can understand that, she said, what's the use of a book like that if one's all set on writing about a nice animal for a newspaper, and at first her husband seemed to agree with her, anyway he didn't object, but then he said that Signor Tartini had especially emphasized that the idea was to concentrate on the description of the animal itself and not be disturbed by the made-up transformation. According to his friend the book dealt with an animal theme in a truly admirable way, which was the reason why he had lent Signor Antonio the book, to give him an opportunity to study it and learn how to cope with an animal of his own choice in writing.

If he were really such a good friend he would've picked another book, Signora Nina said sharply.

What was the animal in the book, my husband asked.

Signor Tartini's book was about an insect, Signora Nina said.

A beetle, Signor Antonio said. But it was just meant to inspire me. I was to choose my own animal.

A beetle, my husband exclaimed.

Exactly so, Signor Antonio confirmed and sounded quite solemn. Just a normal beetle. That surprised you, didn't it?

Well, I'd never have guessed, my husband said, a beetle, and Signor Antonio nodded delightedly, I noticed at once how much this surprised your husband, he said, turning to me, and it seemed that my sweetie's astonishment had provided Signor Antonio with an opportunity to hold forth for longer than usual, now that someone had so unexpectedly shown an interest in what he had to offer, and in detail Signor Antonio began describing the creature in the book his friend had lent him, and with no one interrupting him he spoke of its transparent wings, antennae and several pairs of legs, speaking so well and showing evidence of such talents that I don't believe many of the contributions sent in on the subject of "An Animal Worthy of Our Admiration" could have competed with him, not with this description, so skillful that we felt we could almost see Signor Antonio's animal in front of us; and having talked about the big wings, he now went on to give the beetle another pair of smaller wings in a delicate pale blue color, just behind the big ones, a pair he then gently folded in under the animal's stiff carapace where, although now invisible, they enhanced the insect's ingenious, indeed admirable construction and, with hardly anything missing, completed the image of a beetle in such a way as to almost make me forget that after all this was not a discourse on Signor Antonio's own animal, but the one that belonged to the writer of the little book with the yellow cover lent to him by Signor Tartini, and I saw that Signora Nina's husband had drawn the entire description from memory, without any help from notes.

All this must have been stored inside Signor Antonio's own head without paper and pen getting anywhere near the beetle, and now he carried on, leaving wings and legs behind to describe its eyes and jaws, what kind of temperature and foodstuffs a creature like that prefers and how its digestive system works, and Signor Antonio spoke until Signora Nina interrupted him abruptly and said Toni, I don't think the lady and gentleman have come here to talk about your insect, and then his wife turned to us and said, her words sounding like strokes of a whip, that's the way my husband is, he never gets on with things; and Signor Antonio started and immediately fell silent.

My husband never gets things over and done with, Signora Nina said.

Still engrossed in the world of animals, Signor Antonio heard his sentence being pronounced, delivered by his own wife, and her abrupt judgement made him stop speaking for so long that the whole room filled with the silence, and when Signor Antonio returned to his animal he was stuttering and the beetle was upended on its back. So clumsily had Signor Antonio handled his beetle that it had turned upside-down with its legs in the air.

Or was it the shock rather than his clumsiness? The

brutal frankness that Signora Nina suddenly had allowed herself? Was it his wife who should be blamed, not Signor Antonio, for the beetle now on its back, helplessly waving its six legs in the air?

But after the transformation from human being to beetle not much of importance seemed to be happening in the book that Signor Tartini had lent his friend, and while we had been sitting there listening to Signor Antonio, the heat in the room had become so unbearable that none of us were able to attend to whatever little things might have happened to the animal later on in the story. The beetle no longer interested us as it had before it ended up on its back. Instead, we were beginning to get fed up with his insect even though, after the initial embarrassment, Signor Antonio had pulled himself together and continued the description of the beetle from the point where he had been so rudely interrupted by his wife. But the more details he added, the more unnecessary they seemed, given that the creature, still on its back, was unable to get a move-on. All Signor Antonio's care had been wasted on this beetle. Nothing was of any use, and unwillingly I had to admit to myself that Signora Nina was right; her husband seemed unable to finish anything he started, even in retrospect.

Like the upside-down beetle with its legs in the air he was waving his words in the air without getting anywhere, and I would have liked to turn to him and say that's enough, no, we don't want to listen any more. There was nothing more that I wanted to learn about this creature. But I kept this to myself and went on translating for my husband, although I observed that he too had lost interest in Signor Antonio's entry to the competition "An Animal Worthy of Our Admiration," and now passing the time by eating what was left of the cheese and melon and ham on his plate, and I began to feel sorry for Signora Nina.

This was simply too much.

The description seemed endless, Signor Tartini had obviously lent his book to his friend in vain. Such friendship, and all in vain! Signor Antonio did not even manage to get a beetle over and done with, this tiny animal, in every way so much more modest than a horse and in Signor Tartini's view a suitable creature to inspire his friend, but all in vain; and even the most thoughtful of friends would surely have found it impossible to pick an animal smaller than a beetle, after all friendship also has its rules and limitations, and so Signor Antonio was in the end left alone with this insect of his on which such great expectations had been based, and perhaps for just that reason he had seen no other way out except to now continue with a description that left no fact untold, making the rest of us occupy our minds with whatever else we could think of, anything at all as long as it had nothing to do with his beetle and *Il Piccolo*'s competition "An Animal Worthy of Our Admiration."

Signora Nina had lit her cigarette again and my husband was prodding the remains of ham and lemon on his plate with the fork. Only I had to concentrate on translating for my husband. Out of sheer politeness and compassion we were forcing ourselves to listen to this description, a sense of politeness that had nothing to do with the insect or even Signor Antonio, but everything to do with the empty house, *our* house, with nothing else than the house in Pelegrin.

And still everything had started so hopefully!

What might have become of Signor Antonio's horse would still have interested me. At least in the beginning Signor Tartini's beetle also had promise, that is, before it was turned upside-down, but Signor Antonio couldn't finish even with this little bug, let alone with a whole horse, and his unending struggle for completeness and perfection so utterly beyond his reach must have made Signora Nina's marriage a bitter trial. With growing sympathy I observed her hard, expressionless face that revealed nothing of what was going on in her mind, her black hair, pulled into a bun at the nape of her neck, her thin hands and her red mouth, like a bleeding wound in her face, a woman dressed all in black, all this black of hers seemed to me like the shadow of her husband's illness, and I believed myself to have grasped the most important thing there was to understand about the Baraldi family, the secret of their marriage: that Signora Nina's husband would never be able to finish with his beetle, not even if its legs, one by one, went rigid in the air.

Never would he finish with it, not even if he had had a completely lifeless little insect to inspect, chloroformed and killed, stuck on a pin in a drawer set aside only for totally dead beetles; and his wife, Signora Nina, was aware of this.

Outside in the square the bells chimed five already, and Signor Antonio had got himself stuck in his corner in the company of a creature on its back, no longer of interest to anybody else in the room, a beetle without the slightest chance of competing with all the admirable animals that must once have been put into envelopes marked "An Animal Worthy of Our Admiration" and sent by registered mail to *Il Piccolo*'s offices, a beetle without any capacity at all for inspiring Signor Antonio about an animal of his own, one that could make up for the loss of the dog and the horse, and once more I had to admit that Signora Nina was right.

What kind of friendship was this?

Why had Signor Tartini chosen, of all the animals in the world, to lend his friend a beetle? Had there been no other book about animals on his shelves? Signor Antonio was already seriously ill at the time, his kidneys in the same deadly danger indeed as a beetle on its back, and in his dire need he would have had much more use for a healthy animal, a creature in good shape, not this human being turned beetle provided by his friend, so that I, just like Signora Nina, now came to question if this gesture was truly friendly or if there mustn't be, in all languages, another word to describe what Signor Tartini had done; and while I kept trying to find the right word Signor Antonio continued describing the pitiful state of the beetle on its back, but the more I listened the more I came to believe that what really occupied Signor Antonio's mind was precisely what his wife this Friday afternoon had forbidden him to talk about in front of their guests, the thing he had been told not to speak of, so that he instead had to approach it via the world of animals and his love of animals, all this in order to be able in the end to tell us about this one thing that meant much more to him than beasts of any kind or that empty house in Pelegrin, about the only thing that really preoccupied him—his own severe illness. Of nothing but himself and his own illness was Signor Antonio now speaking, as from his corner he went on detailing the final stages of the overturned beetle's death-agony; and because its fight was Signor Antonio's own, he didn't have the strength to end the story in the only way it could end, not enough courage to bring it to its close. But his wife had seen through him, as she probably sees through everything, and all this I had to keep translating until Signora Nina said Toni, I really don't think the lady and gentleman have come here to talk about your illness.

Her husband had been gesturing with both hands, white palms facing outwards as if Signor Antonio had the white hands of a clown or a baker, but this time he fell silent so very suddenly that we understood that the beetle was gone for good. The room filled with an almost solemn silence; we didn't speak out of a sense of embarrassment that had more to do with Signor Antonio than with the animal in which he'd tried so hard to interest us, though all in vain, and I hoped someone would say something.

So what animal did you decide on in the end, my husband asked.

You and your questions, Signora Nina said, none, Signor Antonio sighed, in the end no animal at all, and Signora Nina looked sternly at him.

Mother was very disappointed, she said, *sì*, her husband said, you let Mother down, Signora Nina said to him, the animals too, Signor Antonio said.

Such a shame, my sweetiepie said.

After that first attempt with the horse nothing seemed to work out properly, Signor Antonio said and sighed again. I let the animals down, he said, my mother too, his wife said, I just gave up, her husband said.

Maybe it wasn't really the right subject for you, my husband said and it was kindly meant. But Signora Nina, who had been assuring us how much her husband loved animals, said nothing; and myself, I just carried on translating.

Just imagine how many animals I've disappointed, Signor Antonio said.

It's such a pity, my sweetie said, and I could see that he really meant it, his eyes were full of compassion for Signor Antonio and the animal that had been denied the chance of a prize in the columns of *Il Piccolo*.

There are so many nice animals in this world of ours, Signor Antonio said, the most interesting being the ones which are most like people in some way, his wife said, and it sounded like a criticism of the beetle even though it had completely vanished by now, but when it came to a choice I just had to make a mistake, Signor Antonio said and sighed, and my husband shook his head in sympathy.

Maybe I should've stayed with the horse, Signor Antonio said, but his wife went on to tell us that the prize-winning entry to *Il Piccolo*'s competition had been anonymous. The person who won the first prize had wished for his name to be kept a secret, but strangely enough he had written about just the same animal that her husband had chosen, that is to say about a horse, just imagine what a coincidence, Signor Antonio said, but a quite different horse from what one might have imagined, Signora Nina said, a horse that had been described in a most poetic and elegant manner, far beyond her husband's abilities; and Signor Antonio was the first one to agree, *un cavallo magnifico,* he said generously, but even so he looked downhearted at this moment, in spite of the many years that had passed since he had failed to get his own contribution ready for the competition "An Animal Worthy of Our Admiration," as if his own, incomplete horse had been stolen from under his very nose.

When the stranger's horse had won the first prize from *Il Piccolo*, Signor Tartini had invited them to a restaurant to console Signor Antonio, a meal with many courses and expensive wines, and even Signora Nina had appreciated this gesture of friendship although it presumably didn't do her husband's kidneys much good.

So thoughtful of Signor Tartini, she said, a true friend in hard times, her husband assured us, but you didn't win, Signora Nina said sharply and Signor Antonio granted that this was true enough, but he'd never thought that a fantasy-horse like that could win a competition held by a highly respectable paper like *Il Piccolo*. The winning horse had reminded him more than anything else of the winged horse that's said to be waiting for poets to leap upon, a horse that doesn't exist in reality and which only poets can ride without falling off, Signor Antonio argued, who himself had never been in the saddle riding a real horse even, and I was translating it all, Pegasus, my sweetie cried, why couldn't you too have used your imagination, Signora Nina said accusingly to her husband.

While listening Signor Antonio had leant forward from his seat in the armchair. The light from the lamp fell from above down on his face and his pale cheeks already looked even bleaker by now, from the light or from a new excitement, no, he said, that's exactly what I couldn't do, he said, no imagination would have helped me.

The three of us, his wife too, looked at him.

No, Signor Antonio repeated, and at this point the light from the lamp made his cheeks look almost yellow, as if the change in the shade of his skin was caused by a hidden yellow tinge underneath his pallor.

It wasn't a whole book of poetry you had to write, Signora Nina said, just a piece for the newspaper, but this time it was her husband who didn't listen; anxiously he was moving back and forth in his armchair and every time he leant forward the light fell on his face, an unnatural glow that for a moment changed the half-light surrounding him, and without the protection of darkness his face was mercilessly exposed to the electric light from the lamp, transforming its human features into a stiff, pale mask, but only for the short moment before Signor Antonio once more shifted back into the shadow again.

He was moving forward and back in the armchair, again and again, and I saw that it was from sheer excitement now, and then he said that people who are ill have no imagination left, none at all—the imagination is what a severe illness destroys first, long before it gets at organs like lungs or kidneys; a really serious illness will always ruin the imagination before starting in on the destruction of the body that houses it, and even if imagination is indeed stronger than reality, it is never as strong as a serious illness.

A serious illness is the one and only exception, Signor Antonio said, and this was why he could never have won a competition like an "An Animal Worthy of Our Admiration," not even with the horse he never finished, not with his already diseased kidneys, not with the kidneys that I don't have any longer, he added to clarify his meaning.

Instead the illness had proved stronger than his intention to describe the horse or the dog or any other animal he had ever admired, because the illness had already wiped out all the imagination he would have needed to meet such a challenge, what nonsense, his wife said, for someone who's ill imagination is actually a deadly poison, Signor Antonio said, don't listen to my husband, Signora Nina said, but her hand shook when she tapped her cigarette out of the holder into the ashtray, though I'm not sure whether she was upset or furious.

What nonsense, she said again, only the one who gives up all hope has a chance of getting well, Signor Antonio said and by now his wife seemed very upset, but I think I understood what he meant: that what is doomed to perish and die can also be kept going quite unnecessarily by hope and imagination.

It takes a really severe illness to force you to be only yourself and nobody else, Signor Antonio said to my husband, as if he'd forgotten that his guest's two kidneys were also of no use and had been replaced by a third and alien one.

A really serious illness cannot be fantasized or dreamt away, it's impossible, and if we tried we'd be totally lost, Signor Antonio said and his wife said Toni, that's enough, but by now there was no stopping her husband, anyone who doesn't believe me had better wait and see what happens when he falls ill himself, he said, *basta*, Signora Nina said crossly, if he hadn't figured it out before this will be the time when he understands that the imagination is the last thing he needs, her husband said, looking rather pleased with his conclusion; and at least for this Signor Antonio had his illness to thank.

And while her husband had been explaining how a severe illness or, at any rate, a severe kidney disease, can destroy everything you need to be successful here in life, Signora Nina had gotten up from the table and started to stack the empty plates to carry them out into the kitchen; there wasn't much left on any of them and nothing at all on my sweetie's plate, only Signor Antonio had hardly touched his ham and melon, and my husband, usually so attentive, was not helping Signora Nina to collect the plates, fascinated by the more philosophical line of thought that Signor Antonio had started to follow after failing absolutely with his beetle, and I wanted to help Signora Nina, but didn't, forced as I was to translate.

Signor Antonio sighed again, but this time it sounded more like a sigh of contentment, having been able to dominate the conversation for such a long time, and with my husband at least for one interested listener.

You weren't so ill then, Signora Nina said, but I didn't feel well, her husband said, you only fell really ill when you retired from the Post Office, she replied, he's so stubborn, she went on after having turned to us, what do you mean, stubborn, Signor Antonio asked, the way you behaved in Pisa, Signora Nina said, though you never did get to the top of the tower, I did, her husband said, *no*, Signora Nina said, *si*, her husband said, and everything they said to each other I tried to translate until my husband said wait, is it supposed to be yes or no, and neither of them understood what my husband had said and Signor Antonio repeated what he had just said, *si*, he said, but his wife insisted on her no, *no*, she said, and my husband turned to me and said make up your mind, is it yes or no, so I had to turn to Signor and Signora Baraldi and explain to them that my husband was confused, not understanding why one of them says yes and the other no, as he doesn't speak Italian.

Si, capisco, Signor Antonio said and looked at my husband as if he would have liked to help him out by saying this, *capisco,* he said again and waved amiably at my husband from his corner, but Signora Nina who had just sat down at the table immediately got up again, it cannot go on like this, she said, *no,* Signor Antonio said, what is she saying, my husband asked, why don't you translate what she says, he went on, and now Signora Nina too had turned to me and I could see that she was upset.

We'll never get anywhere unless you make up your mind to translate only the most important points for your husband, Signora Nina said, *si, appunto,* Signor Antonio said, only what's most important, nothing else, Signora Nina insisted. It's almost six o'clock. The whole afternoon has passed and we still haven't dealt with business matters, she continued and her husband agreed with her, time waits for no one, he said and shook his head, here we're on Italian soil, and the language is good enough for us, Signora Nina said, Italian will do for us, and I had not had enough time to translate anything of this, but my sweetie still looked quite pleased, as if from what he actually didn't understand at all he had understood that we were getting closer to the house at last, to *our* house, and your husband not being able to understand what's said has little to do with the house in Pelegrin and our business deal, Signora Nina said.

We'll get nowhere if everything that's said is translated as well, but if you still insist I must ask you to use as much discretion as possible, she told me, only the most important things, Signor Antonio said, I really must ask you not to waste our time more than absolutely necessary, Signora Nina said to me, we all want to get this house business settled as soon as we can, don't we, time waits for no one, her husband said from his corner, I mean you've come to Trieste on business, haven't you, Signora Nina said, and I had to admit that she was right, nothing but the empty house in Pelegrin had brought us to Trieste; and Signora Nina shrugged her shoulders as if she had known all along that she was right and didn't need anyone to confirm it.

If you think about it you'll find that everything you translate for your husband has already been said and I hardly think we've got time for that, she said, instead of getting to the heart of the matter we're just wasting time on repetition, Signora Nina said, just in vain, Signor Antonio said, we've all got things to do, his wife said, and I tried to compress what had been said into a few brief sentences for my husband who hadn't understood any of it.

All he knew was that this Italian conversation had moved across the border into Istria and was on its way up to Pelegrin, so in spite of not grasping the meaning of the Italian words he still must have felt more at home, now that we were approaching the empty house, and the most important thing was that it was the Baraldis and not me who, using all these incomprehensible Italian words, had finally brought the house into the conversation, and for that insight he needed no translation.

What a pleasant way of whiling away the time sitting here talking to you, Signor Antonio said, but Signora Nina looked at her husband at length without speaking, and then started to collect the plates that were still on the table and went to the kitchen for the second time. Only the large platter with ham and cheese and melon was still there on the table, and when she returned she brought two clean plates and put them in front of my husband and me.

But the silence she had left behind in the room had been as stern and reproachful as Signora Nina herself and none of us had got round to breaking it, so that now returning from the kitchen she found it in the same state as when she had left, a silence as unrelenting as Signor Antonio's shut Post Office window, with the message that any objections or protests would not reach their intended addressee.

We were all waiting for what Signora Nina had to say. Signor Antonio could not count on being listened to anymore, not on the subject of animals or his illness, and after coming back from the kitchen his wife remained standing behind her chair instead of sitting down at the table again; there she stood, stern and black, just as she had been at the beginning of the afternoon when she had asked us to be seated at the table.

This is a very complicated matter, Signora Nina said and her husband nodded. It was now quite obvious that what she was speaking of now had nothing to do with our earlier conversations, only with the empty house in Pelegrin, with nothing else.

The matter is indeed more complicated than anyone could believe, Signora Nina said, but we have come to the conclusion that we can sell you the house for one hundred million lire.

How much, my sweetie whispered.

One hundred million, I whispered back, and under the tablecloth I reached for his left hand and held it, the scabs on his cuts still felt rough and Signor Antonio waved kindly to us from his armchair, but took care that his wife wouldn't notice.

We've been told that we should set the initial price at one hundred and ten million lire, Signora Nina continued, so you could then negotiate a ten million reduction and we'd arrive at the one hundred we want anyway. But then, how could I know that you wouldn't carry on and try for ninety-five or even ninety, encouraged by the ten we'd already given you though we really haven't, as we'd never counted on that much in the first place, just added them to the hundred that we actually want for the sole purpose of making it look better, from your point of view that is, Signora Nina said, because then you might believe that you'd saved ten million lire, which would however not be the case as we had never actually counted upon the higher price but simply the price I told you at the outset, that is, the lower one. Strictly speaking we're therefore speaking about ten million which is of no importance whatsoever for our negotiations and personally I cannot see the point of first demanding that sum from you only so that we would then be able to give it back to you, money that doesn't actually exist. That's why my husband and I have decided to fix the price at one hundred million, Signora Nina said. So that we don't have to go on haggling over the deal.

While Signora Nina had been holding forth about the price of the house, my husband had been looking as if he were really trying to understand what she was saying, even scattering some of his Italian words here and there as comments, but in the wrong places, and nodding his head when he should have been shaking it, and so I said to Signora Nina that my husband and I would have to think about their offer first, but promised to let them know as soon as possible, and at this statement too my husband shook his head, he'd understood nothing at all.

That's all right, Signor Antonio said and nodded agreement from his armchair, sounding rather as if it was he who had bought the house, *our* house, from under our noses, and Signora Nina began dishing out melon and cheese and ham again on the clean plates, my sweetie said *mille grazie* and started eating again with good appetite. But of Signora Nina's discourse he hadn't understood a single word, at most one or two odd figures, and turning to Signor Antonio he said that in this way there would surely be enough money to spare for a proper kidney transplant, perhaps even done in America where the best kidneys and the best doctors are, a well-known fact, and I translated it all and Signor Antonio nodded and seemed very pleased, *America*, he said, a real kidney, my husband added while serving himself some more ham, but Signora Nina had taken all this in and said that there was no question of anything of the kind; a transplant would be far too expensive, what's she saying, my husband asked, but I didn't translate that for him.

We seem to have settled the matter then, Signora Nina said, and there was no mistaking that she was referring to the house again and not her husband's illness, what is she saying, my husband asked, chewing on his ham, we'd better arrange to meet as soon as possible at the house so we can hand over the keys, Signora Nina said to us. Even if you two want time to think, it can do no harm to look the house over. So that you can inspect what you've bought.

By then twilight was gathering. Summer afternoons like this hardly have time to start before they're over and the room was full of anxious shadows, taller and thinner now than just a couple of hours ago, but time is the last thing one thinks about on such summer afternoons. The heat was enveloping Trieste like a white shroud. The fierce heat had transformed the city, usually so familiar, turning it into something out of reach, but at the same time bringing alarmingly close things that we usually manage to keep at arms-length; and whoever is able to will flee as far away as they can from heat like this, but none of us had had the strength, all we could do was stay hidden behind closed shutters, and outside the square must have been empty. In such heat no one could be moving across it, only the day was moving, passing away and the evening was closing in, on such hot summer afternoons nothing but time can keep on the move and time had now merged with the heat and disappeared, though still allowing nothing to interfere with its passage, as gray or white as the heat itself, so that time and heat could not be kept apart, not that we even tried, who would have had the strength?

So we'll meet in Pelegrin the next time, my husband said.

But Signor Antonio waved both his hands as if he were not particulary interested in going visiting.

My wife was always more attached to the house than I am, he said, what nonsense, Signora Nina said, my husband just loved the house in Pelegrin, but Signor Antonio stood by what he had said and told us that he certainly wouldn't mourn the house though it now was no longer theirs, and also that it had never meant that much to him. You loved the house and always looked after it, his wife said, but Signor Antonio just shook his head at this, how could I have been looking after it when I was never there? We were hardly ever there, he went on, what nonsense, Signora Nina said, but her husband stood by what he'd said, love was out of the question, who could love a house; according to Signora Nina's husband it was unreasonable to become attached to something that is just lent to you, and, besides, he'd never much cared for the house in Pelegrin, such silly talk, his wife said, but Signor Antonio insisted, it had made him nervous simply to think of the house being there in the same place all the time, and also he had always felt ill at ease indoors, not even playing billiards had kept him amused, but you did play, Signora Nina said, hardly ever, he said, my husband often played billiards with Signor Tartini in the house in Pelegrin, his wife said to my husband, who plays neither billiards nor cards, I always hoped that we'd arrive in Pelegrin and the house wouldn't be there, Signor Antonio said, at least once, what nonsense, his wife said sternly, how could a whole house suddenly disappear, and without even sitting down at the table she'd in this way dealt with both billiards and the house, and was ready to start on more practical matters now.

Signora Nina asked if we had a lawyer who could draft the contract and set out the correct information for the Property Register in Buzet, but only after we had settled the matter with the purchase sum, to be paid in five installments of two hundred thousand lire each, paid into Signora Nina's account in the Trieste branch of their bank, but when I told her that my husband and I must discuss this in peace and quiet first, and rashly mentioned the name of my lawyer Signora Nina pursed her lips, a *Hochstapler*, she said, and this single German word sounded ominous among all the Italian ones.

Who's she talking about, my husband asked, he's tried to get his hands on that house for years, Signora Nina said, who is this, my husband asked again, that man claims to have papers and documents to show that it doesn't belong to us, Signora Nina said, and I didn't know what to think; at least as far as I knew and even though he'd lost my insurance papers the other day, advocate Franjo had behaved perfectly properly about managing my own house, though it's too small for my sweetiepie.

A *Hochstapler*, Signora Nina repeated, that's what he is. He hasn't even got his own papers in order, she added, is it your man Laginja she's talking about, my husband asked, as if your communists would have allowed advocates with real degrees, Signora Nina said and turned to her husband in his corner for confirmation.

Anyway, I'm pleased we're rid of it, Signor Antonio said to his wife, I never liked that house, and it wasn't easy to work out if he had always held this opinion or if that's what he had started to feel once he and his wife had decided to sell, let's meet on Sunday, Signora Nina said, we'll be coming to look after our graves anyhow, Signor Antonio said.

After Mass, Signora Nina said when we said goodbye.

It was already dark when we drove back from Trieste to Pelegrin. In the darkness we had to wait in the lines at the borders, together with the Slovenian and Croatian guest-workers on their way home for the weekend, first lining up at the border between the largest and the smallest nations, and then on the border between the smallest and the somewhat bigger one, and all this waiting and all these borders, crammed into the smallest possible space, is something we Istrians have to live with, but every time my sweetiepie gets annoyed, both with the waiting and with the borders.

Like dogs lifting a leg to mark out their territory, he says and it's us, living here in Istria and our borders that he's talking about, this constant pissing all over the place, he rumbles on, this idiotic form of nationalistic cystitis, and it doesn't help to tell him that we Istrians don't take any notice of the borders and feel united even though we have to wait, because he doesn't listen.

Just like dogs marking their territory, my husband says who is not from this part of the world, in this place you get pissed on from all directions, he says, but this Friday he fell asleep from the wine and the long Trieste afternoon which was just as well as I wasn't in the mood for trying to find out what we'd actually agreed with the Baraldis, I was too tired, and my husband would not have been of any help; only at the border checkpoints he woke up to show his passport, and the journey back took much longer than the drive from Pelegrin to Trieste that morning.

The twilight was deepening and the nearer we got to home, the emptier and more desolate were the roads, and the ruts and potholes were telling me that this really was the way back home. Flickering lights glowed here and there in the dark, hazy in the heat, on its fifth day now and lingering inside the darkness, but just a few lights in the crumbling and almost completely deserted villages with neither wells nor electricity, and behind us in the blackness of the night the lower edge of the sky was faintly illuminated by the many lights of Trieste. This rim of light on the horizon was all that was left of the city, now hidden behind the mountains and hills of Istria, down there a dim glow emanated from the city of Trieste, crowded in between the mountains and the sea, and as we climbed the last steep hillsides up towards Pelegrin the beams from the car's headlights for a moment swept across the sky, a sky without moon or stars, and my sweetiepie slept.

He only came to life once I had parked the car behind the house and switched off the headlights, he yawned and went ahead of me into the house. I watered the vegetable plot in the light from the lamp above the door. Large insects were dancing around the lamp, bumping against the glass, and when I had finished my husband had already gone to bed and fallen asleep again.

I gently closed the bedroom door and went to the kitchen to get myself a cup of tea. But before I had time to start heating the water, someone knocked lightly on the front door, a very light knock once and then once more on the small glass window of the door, and when I went to find out who it was, Dimitrij was standing just outside in the dark with a parcel under his arm, something flat and square wrapped in newspaper.

Can I come in, Dimitrij asked.

It was late and pitch-dark outside, but I let him into

the kitchen where we would disturb my husband less than if we had gone into our other room. Dimitrij put down what he had brought and I asked him to have a seat. He smiled at me and settled at the kitchen table, and his smile was the one Dimitrij has ready for everyone without ever letting it belong to anybody in particular, a smile for himself alone and for his suspicions of everything, more like a grin than a smile, the same smile as on our Monday visit to his house.

Between these two smiles of Dimitrij's four days had passed, but his smile on Friday night was the same smile as on Monday night, a smile in order to gain time although he was no longer in his own house but in my little one, and the time Dimitrij was claiming with his smile was not his but mine, *my* time under *my* roof, and he looked around the kitchen curiously, taking his time, and then lifted and examined the things on the kitchen table in front of him; the salt cellar, the corkscrew, a teaspoon, and if he had gone on to pocket the spoon, I'd have just let it happen.

All right if I smoke, Dimitrij asked, still with the same smile on his face, and without waiting for an answer he produced a cigarette from his breast pocket and put it between his lips, still behaving as if he had plenty of time and was considering staying a while there, in *my* kitchen, even though his own house is just a stone's throw away, that frightened me, and my husband was asleep.

Dimitrij lit his cigarette and his eyes and mouth looked as if they didn't belong on the same face, the bleary eyes in the upper half didn't fit with the mouth and its insolent smile in the lower, two odd halves put together into one face, but a face that is all he owns apart from a drawer full of photographs, this face that has got nothing to do with our village or with any other village in our neighborhood, looking as if it had been put together halfway between two places and wouldn't be welcome in either one, but least of all could such a face belong here in Pelegrin, and every time Dimitrij walks through the village his face is bound to remind us that he isn't one of us, even though Dimitrij himself insists on the opposite, but with a face like that he's quite helpless here, nothing but a stranger; and he knows this, that it is his face that has been giving him away, and so this truculent and cunning expression has taken over, the only thing about him which has had its origin here with us, and now he was with me in my kitchen.

I've never come visiting you before, he said and smiled and what he said was as true as it was unpleasant.

Even though his house is only a stone's throw away from ours, he has never set foot here, but the smile on his face was even more disturbing than what he had said, a smile that belonged to another face than his eyes, we've never had an invitation of course, Dimitrij said, still smiling, my wife and I wouldn't suit fine people like yourselves, and to that I had nothing to say, I stayed silent.

We are just not good enough for this little house and now your husband wants to buy himself a bigger one, Dimitrij said and blew cigarette smoke across the kitchen table, and I had nothing to say to that either, but now I'm here, Dimitrij said, and his smile had become self-confident and malicious, no longer a smile for gaining time.

Though in fact time was something he seemed to have plenty of and his having so much time on his hands in the middle of the night worried me. It was late, my husband was asleep and there was too much truth in what he had said; we had never invited Dimitrij and his wife for anything, not even a coffee or a glass of grappa. But my husband would never ask him, not even as Dimitrij Borejko, son of the Inspector General and grandson of Major Borejko, that much I knew and so did Dimitrij.

We'd better keep our voices down, I said. My husband is asleep.

I was trying to stay as still as possible, speaking in a whisper so as not to disturb the peace and quiet and wake my husband, who, after his long, strenuous afternoon in Trieste, was sleeping in the room on the other side of the kitchen, and now Dimitrij too spoke in a low voice, lower than my own, something that made me even more nervous than when he had been loud enough to possibly wake my husband. Dimitrij's subdued, intimate voice in the middle of the night frightened me, it sounded as if Dimitrij and I were sharing a secret, so I spoke up.

Dimitrij, I said more loudly than before, but he only kept smiling and lowered his voice still more, I hope I'm not disturbing you, he whispered and glanced curiously around the kitchen.

By now he didn't want to lose the intimacy of our whispered conversation and our two voices were almost indistinguishable, though it frightened me to be speaking so quietly with someone I was forbidden to have anything to do with, but Dimitrij had gained the upper hand.

Dimitrij, I whispered, it's late, and he stood up at once as if he really intended to go back to his own home.

But instead he started walking about in my little kitchen, looking around as if he had all the time in the world, you know, I've never been here before, he said while he was smiling at me.

Dimitrij, I whispered but instead of answering he went over to the window and the sink; he picked up the flour jar and put it back, then the sugar bowl and the pepper-mill, touched the curtains, smiling all the time, a little wry smile meant for no one in particular, like the smile of a blind person, and then he got hold of the spatula from the frying pan on the stove, twisted and turned it and then the salad tongs, before he put them back in the sink, and all the time he was smiling at me.

Dimitrij, I said, but not loudly enough, it was little more than a whisper, and Dimitrij picked up the bread knife and inspected it though there was no bread around, Dimitrij, I whispered, what is that you want, but Dimitrij wasn't listening, just standing there with the knife in his hand.

Cautiously he tried the tip of the knife against his index finger and when he started walking again, around the kitchen table where I was sitting stock-still, he held on to the knife. Like an animal he padded about in my kitchen, but one quite unlike the domestic animals we'd devoted so much time talking about that afternoon in Trieste, not like any of Signor Antonio's pets, and behind my back Dimitrij was speaking to me, you and I are the only people in Pelegrin who understand each other, he whispered, you and I, and as he said "each other" he must have stopped just behind my back, and at that moment I feared more than anything else that he would put his hand on my shoulder or stroke my hair; the knife didn't frigthen me, only his hand on my shoulder or my hair.

But nothing happened and suddenly Dimitrij was standing in front of me again.

Then he sat down at my husband's usual place at the kitchen table and now he was no longer smiling. He just looked at the bread knife as if wondering what it was doing there in his hand, and then he put it down on the table.

The two of us must stick together, Dimitrij said.

His face was made up of two halves that had been joined but didn't belong with each other, just as day and night never more than touch each other even though they share a twenty-four hour span, a face that would never become merged into a whole, but now Dimitrij was no longer smiling and I wasn't frightened any more.

There was nothing about this face to make me afraid any longer. Without that smile, Dimitrij's eyes dominated his face and everything that had appeared brutal and suspicious had vanished with the smile; what remained was a blank face looking almost lifeless, but with nothing to hide.

You're like one of us, Dimitrij said.

You don't dislike me, he said, looking at the bread knife on the table in front of him.

My husband has nothing against you, Dimitrij, I whispered, but he only shook his head.

No one here wishes me well, Dimitrij said and now he wasn't whispering any longer.

That's not true, Dimitrij.

Do you mind if I smoke, he asked, and I turned to reach for the ashtray on the windowsill so that he wouldn't drop ash on our kitchen table any longer. He smoked in silence, looking at me.

Please, I said to Dimitrij, you must pull yourself together.

I know, he said. But I need a success.

We all strive for things, I said.

I know.

But it's not enough to know. What one knows one also has to try to carry out.

I do try, he said, and his eyes were fixed on the bread knife, or at least that's what it seemed like, as if the knife were the only thing on the table that interested him.

Is that really true, Dimitrij?

Everybody here is against me.

Surely it's not that bad, I said. I can't believe that.

You know nothing, Dimitrij said. If only you knew

what I know. But your husband knows something about the empty house that nobody else knows.

What could he know, I said. My husband doesn't come from here.

Perhaps that's why. Sooner or later the Italians are going to take their property back. The houses belong to them anyway, Dimitrij said. But I can't do anything about that, this village is not my place. I'm just a Borejko.

Dimitrij, please, I said, you really must pull yourself together. Do you know what time it is?

I'll be on my way, he replied hurriedly, but the very same words which calmed me must have made him remember what he was doing here in the first place, and he looked down at the parcel he had brought, on the floor propped up against the leg of the kitchen table, and just as he had lit his first cigarette without asking my permission, he now started unwrapping his parcel as if I weren't there. It contained something flat and square, and once the paper was off I saw that it was the portrait of his grandfather Major Borejko, the picture that had been on the wall in Dimitrij's house, but was now on my kitchen table.

I thought you might like to buy it, Dimitrij said. It's by Vrkljan.

I could see at once that your husband liked this picture, he said and then went on to explain that he had planned to sell the picture to a museum but changed his mind once he realized how much the picture meant to my husband.

I noticed straightaway that your husband is a man of taste, Dimitrij said, and I didn't want to hurt him, but still felt I had to mention that the picture after all was a portrait of Dimitrij's own grandfather, a close relative, and that without it he would have even less of his family left, but Dimitrij just shrugged his shoulders.

You could buy the picture as a gift, a surprise for your husband, he said.

I really don't know. I must ask him first. But it will have to wait until tomorrow.

There's nobody else in Pelegrin with good taste, Dimitrij said, and I assured him that it was a very fine picture, but still I had to think about it until tomorrow.

A real Vrkljan. But I'd want the frame back. The painting is for sale. Not the frame.

It's a very fine painting, Dimitrij, I said. But I really don't know.

Can you understand how I feel, Dimitrij suddenly said, and now he had lowered his voice to a whisper again. You only come here in the summer. People like you come and go as you please. But I have to stay here. I'll never get away from here. I've grown to be a part of this dreadful place.

My husband wants to buy the empty house and live here year round, I said. You know that very well, Dimitrij, but he didn't look as if he'd heard what I said.

Your husband is not from here either, he said, as if this sufficiently explained both his own and my husband's fate.

I'm sure my husband doesn't know more about the

empty house that anybody else, I said. To tell you the truth, I don't think he knows anything much about it at all, but he's fallen in love with it. And only with that house, no other will do. He wants it at any price. But if he does manage to buy it he'll probably want to have his own relatives on the wall and not your grandfather.

What difference does that make, Dimitrij asked, but either he had given up on the idea of selling the picture to me or he really trusted my husband's good taste and truly wanted me to have time to speak to him about it, because Dimitrij now started wrapping up Major Borejko in newspaper again; some of the creased pages had fallen on the floor and he bent to pick them up.

In this village it would be better for your husband to have my grandfather on the wall rather than his own, he said. It would make things easier for him.

But Dimitrij, it's your family.

What does it matter, he said and by now he had finished wrapping the picture again. It doesn't matter at all. I believe you and I can be frank with each other.

No, I said, we can't.

As you wish, Dimitrij said. But are you sure that your husband has his own grandfather in oil? Anyway, it won't be a real Vrkljan. You can be sure of that. He won't have a real Vrkljan.

I didn't want to hurt you, Dimitrij, I said. Have I hurt you?

He had risen from the table and stood there with his parcel stuck under his arm, hesitating and looking down, this difficult moment when disappointment had not yet acquired the hard, impenetrable shell that makes for safe-keeping, but maybe he wasn't even disappointed; perhaps disappointment is something people like Dimitrij cannot allow themselves, at least not for long.

It doesn't matter, he said.

Please Dimitrij, I hope you're not angry with me?

No, he said. But it really doesn't matter.

Are you sure?

Yes, he said. I'm sure. It doesn't matter.

I opened the door for him and outside it was dark, a black night without any stars, and already halfway into the darkness, on his way back to his own house, he turned in the doorway.

Goodnight, Dimitrij, I said, and with his grandfather tightly under his arm, he said something to me that I didn't catch and had to ask him to repeat.

We need rain, Dimitrij said. A lot of rain.

THEN SUNDAY CAME, THE WEEK was over and the church-bell called people to Mass, but no one arrived from Trieste, nor did anyone turn up after Mass. My husband paced up and down under the three great trees next to the church, then went into our house to check that the telephone was working, and next he was back out there again, but it was only late in the afternoon, when we had begun to worry about a possible accident, that Signora Nina and Signor Antonio drove into Pelegrin. The sun was already setting. They parked outside Beppo's house and Beppo was there, shaved and wearing a clean white shirt, still sober, even though Bruno's inn had long been open by then.

Signor Antonio was all soaked in sweat when he climbed out of the car and before giving himself time to close the car door, he started explaining that their last visit to Pelegrin was so long ago that his wife had forgotten the road and taken a wrong turn, not just once but several times. They had wandered off as far as Grimalda and Senj, and only there had they turned round and driven back towards Buzet, but overshot it, and just below Motovun his wife had almost run over some hens and might have killed them; two hens had run across the road from left to right and when she had made way for them suddenly a third one appeared, a third hen that got hit by the car, and there really was some white down smeared on the bumper in congealed blood, but thank goodness, the impact was slight, Signor Antonio assured us, all three hens must have got away, and Signora Nina was in an excellent mood, wearing black net gloves in spite of the heat.

In a loud voice she ordered Beppo to fetch the keys to the house, such useful little animals, Signor Antonio said, but his wife wasn't interested in hens any longer, give me the keys, Signora Nina said to Beppo, making it sound like an order, and Beppo hurried off into his house and came back with a key-ring with three keys.

None of these keys looked at all like the wrought iron one he had handed over to my husband three days ago, and my sweetie stared angrily at him, but Signora Nina said that we should get going at once, the house is waiting, and almost speaking across her, my husband repeated what she had said.

Let's go, he said, no time to lose, the house is waiting, and I saw how excited he was, as if he wouldn't be able to hold himself in check for much longer. To celebrate this moment he had put on a tie, red with white lilies, which I felt sure I'd never seen before; I had no idea where that tie came from and I too felt strangely elated, almost solemn, as Signora Nina started walking ahead of us along the gravel path between the inn's wine cellar and the ruin in front of Beppo's house, towards the wall of the empty one, and using the biggest of the keys she unlocked the gate in the wall so that I could step into the garden and see for myself what was on the other side; but what I now saw in there, on the other side of the wall for the first time, was more than disappointing.

The garden was a wilderness. It was overshadowed by four huge bay trees, probably as old as the house, and once on this side of the wall, the grounds seemed smaller than I had imagined from the outside. Parts of the bay trees had died, but no one had cut down the whitened branches and tidied them away; instead the storms must have taken off some of the withered wood, though to work out whether it had been done by summer or by winter storms was not possible. The broken branches with their stiff, brown leaves lay scattered in the long grass, and here and there large patches of lawn had been burnt away by the sun. Everything growing inside the garden walls seemed out of control, dark and wild vegetation in complete disorder, ivy was even climbing up the orchard trees, stunted little fruit trees, mostly plums and cherries, growing in the shadow of the bay trees, and looking more like big shrubs than real trees.

The day's last light fell on the garden and the empty house, which at close range looked more run down than from the other side of the wall, from *our* side of it. Here and there were patches of flaking paint on the facade that showed the plaster underneath, and the color of the paint was *rosso romano,* but in that pale brick-red there were damp areas of darker red. By now the sun was setting rapidly, but in its fading light I could still read the text carved on a stone plaque above the entrance door of the house: LAVS DEO ANNO 1772 P. M. B. F. F. DIE 22 MAY, letters and figures cut into the stone over two hundred years ago, and when Signora Nina also unlocked the front door and asked us to enter, a stale cellar smell hit us as we stepped into the dim half-light of the house.

There's no light, Signora Nina said, and Signor Antonio wiped his face with a white handkerchief and nodded, a very old house without electricity, he said, but my husband said nothing at all, he was nervously scratching at the almost healed wounds in his hands and I didn't have the slightest idea of what might be going on inside his head, if anything at all; my husband seemed completely preoccupied with his hands while Signora Nina pulled a small flashlight from her handbag and began walking ahead of us into the house. We now followed her into a large, empty hall and my husband gave up trying to restrain himself, his excitement was brimming over and he kept scratching at the scabs on his hands.

The house too disappointed me. Inside it was divided along a north-south axis into nine very large rooms on three floors, and all nine rooms were covered in dust. One room opened into the next, each one no larger and no smaller than the others, and each floor was exactly alike, offering no distinctions between one floor and another, and in every one room the shutters were closed so that all nine rooms were filled with darkness; only the day's last light was seeping in from outside, strained through the slats of the shutters, a faint daylight falling on gray or white floorboards, white or gray as the inner walls of the house, even though it was almost too dark to see any colors at all; and furniture under cloth covers stood in each room as if a very long time ago someone had put the pieces in their places and left the room without any intention of even returning, and the covers too were covered by dust, covers in the same colors as the walls and floors, so that everything in the rooms was either white or gray; everything in this house was coated with dust and in the last light from the day outside, a light that still was coming in through the slatted shutters, the dust was hovering slowly in the air before being swallowed up by the dark once more, and again and again Signor Antonio wiped his face with his white handkerchief although the air inside the house was neither hot nor damp, but rather dry, and almost chilly.

All the time Signora Nina walked ahead of us, always entering a new room first so that when we reached it she could turn round ready to tell us what kind of room it was. This is the winter kitchen, Signora Nina would be saying, or this is the bedroom, this is the hall, or in here used to be the billiard table, and all of it I translated as exactlly as I could for my husband, and when Signora Nina had led the way up a narrow stair from the hall into a much smaller space, darker than the other nine rooms and really more like a large closet than a proper room, she turned to us and said that once there'd been a bathtub in here once, a real tin tub but not any longer, but by then my sweetiepie had already walked up to the wall at the far end of the room and was tapping on it.

Look at your husband, Signora Nina said to me. He's already moved in.

But my sweetie was tapping on the wall again as if he were looking for something in it, a cavity perhaps or an emergency exit, maybe even an opening to a secret passage, as if expecting somebody on the other side would open up a door and ask him to enter in the same way as Signora Nina had asked us all to enter the empty house in her company, to enter *our* house, and then my sweetie put his ear to the wall while he kept knocking on it.

Over and over he tapped and listened.

By now we were all watching him and Signor Antonio kept wiping his white handkerchief across his face, the sweat pouring down the back of his neck and over his forehead, flowing in such streams that everyone could see that Signora Nina had told us nothing but the truth right from the start of our visit to Trieste, that her husband was very sick indeed, but then suddenly my husband stopped tapping, turned to me and said translate, and I translated.

My husband says that this wall must come down, I said.

The room became totally silent.

One could hear a solitary blackbird singing in the garden, and then Signora Nina said come down, why?

But my husband didn't answer, just kept mumbling to himself. I don't think he any longer saw or heard the rest of us, and the moon came to my mind again, the fat moon that maddens people and cattle here in Istria, and then my husband said that's right, the wall must come down.

What's the point, Signora Nina said.

Her voice was irritated and at the same time guarded, but I too couldn't understand why that wall had to go unless it was to make the room larger and get enough space for a proper bathtub, built in with tiles, not one of those free-standing tin tubs on clawed feet, and all the time my husband was looking straight into Signora Nina's eyes as if she were the one person there who would understand every word he was saying, although she could understand nothing until I translated it for her, *non capsico niente*, Signora Nina said, and my husband went on staring at her, behaving as if the two of them were alone in the room and as if only she, Signora Nina, understood precisely what he was talking about.

That's right, my sweetiepie said to her. I'm going to demolish that wall.

Impossibile, Signora Nina said. It's out of the question.

The wall must go, my husband said. It must be taken down.

No, Signora Nina said.

If it's all right with everybody I'll go and take a turn in the garden, Signor Antonio said, and his voice sounded very faint. But his wife, whom he was actually addressing, said *no*, there can be no question of tearing the wall down, *proprio impossibile*. In a house like this you can't start pulling down whatever you please, just because you want to get rid of a wall or to find out what might be on the other side of it, even if it cannot be completely ruled out that at some point in time someone else might have shared your husband's opinion, Signora Nina went on, now speaking directly to me just as my husband earlier had addressed her alone, that someone at some point in time might have considered tearing down a whole wall in this house, maybe even the one in front of us now, Signora Nina said and pointed her flashlight at the wall that my sweetie had been tapping on, but even so it's easy to see that in any case the person must have thought better of it. The wall is still there. Can you, please, explain that to your husband.

This wall must go, my sweetie said, starting to tap on it again with his knuckles, and Signora Nina crossed her arms over her chest; her black net gloves didn't show up any longer in the darkness, only her bare white arms seemed to glow, looking paler and more naked than before.

How could it be any other way, Signora Nina went on, and though what she had said sounded like a question it no longer seemed directed at anyone in particular.

Signora Nina had switched off the flashlight so that we were standing together in the dark, and turning to me she said that surely no one could fail to grasp that if first *one* wall is demolished, then another one will be taken down next and still others will follow, so that soon there'll be no inner walls left in the house, and in the end no house at all. At least nothing looking like a proper house, the way this one does, Signora Nina said, a house I am trying to show you to the best of my ability, a house your husband has practically bought already, this very house and none other, and if we had allowed it to look whichever way we might have fancied at the time, well, then your husband would soon have been the owner of something quite different from what he first thought he had bought, Signora Nina said to me and switched the flashlight on again, but my husband said nothing.

That wouldn't be in anybody's interest, least of all ours, Signora Nina said, and searched with her eyes for her husband, who had stayed with us in the bathroom although he had asked his wife to be allowed to go out into the garden.

Isn't that so, Toni, Signora Nina said, and Signor Antonio nodded while he squeezed his handkerchief between his hands, under no circumstances, he said. Besides, Signora Nina said to me, if this wall were really unnecessary then your husband must explain to me how it came to be built here in the first place and how it's managed to stay untouched for over two hundred years. Now, can he explain that to me? Because I can't imagine that your husband would try to argue that the wall isn't really there, Signora Nina said, and now she directed the flashlight towards the wall, almost exactly at the spot where my husband had been knocking on it with his knuckles, and the light on the wall formed a perfect circle of pale yellow light surrounded by blackness, just like the full moon in August in our Istrian night sky.

Please translate all that I have said to your husband, Signora Nina told me.

But before I had time to start translating we heard a voice coming out of the darkness below in the hall; someone must have entered the house through the open door without our noticing, and someone cried is anybody there, and that someone was Father Sverko, our priest.

God be with you, the priest said when he stepped into the room where we all were staying as if frozen to the spot by the darkness, and then he pulled a handful of cherries from the right-hand pocket on his cassock and held them out for us to eat, a whole handful of dark red, almost black cherries, which glowed faintly in the dark, but only Signor Antonio was interested in the offering; he bowed to the priest and took some cherries from the outstretched hand.

It's the last cherries of the year, Father Sverko said, but it was difficult to hear what the priest was saying as quite a few of the cherries he was talking about were in his mouth.

The garden is full of cherries but these are the last ones for this summer, the priest went on, but never mind, soon we'll have the joy of ripe figs too, and my husband had stopped tapping on the wall, but hadn't even greeted the priest, and to me he muttered that he couldn't recall inviting any priests to eat his fruit, not here in *our* garden, but I didn't translate that.

I was beginning to feel tired of being the only translator all the time. Outside the day was now drawing to an end, the afternoon was soon to become evening, the garden would turn dark and gloomy, and while I was translating I had the feeling that no one was actually listening to me, that instead everyone was engaged with nothing but their own words, never giving a thought to how difficult it was for me to find some that matched all of theirs, but in quite a different language, trying to keep the flow of original words meaningful also for those who could not immediately understand them; an almost impossible task, so that every word I struggled to replicate as faithfully as possible was not of much use and often rather irritated the speakers or caused misunderstandings, like when my husband didn't recognize his own words in Italian, and that's why I'd started leaving out more and more of what was being said.

They all seemed so pleased with what they'd expressed in their own language that they didn't seem to care what became of it in another one, a language they

RICHARD SWARTZ

didn't understand anyway, and therefore I started to compress what seemed too long and complicated, and nobody noticed; only what they themselves said seemed important to them, and instead of translating what had already been said I began to change their words into what I felt that they ought to have said, not in order to twist the meaning, but helping to make it clearer, for the common good, taking care that no one should become disappointed or annoyed with anyone else, and for this task there was no one else around but me, and in most cases with no opinions of my own; and Father Sverko was explaining how cherries are at their very best towards the end of the summer, just before they start to rot, and that he'd brought the cherries in from the garden.

The garden gate had been open of course, the priest said with his mouth full of cherries, from the church I spotted a strange light inside the house, an uncertain light, waxing and waning. Behind the shutters one room after another on the upper floors was lit up as if by flames, the priest said. I thought the house was on fire.

You thought the whole place was going up in flames, Signor Antonio said, but what the priest had been watching from the church must have been the beam of Signora Nina's flashlight, and Signor Antonio sighed, or perhaps it was a sob, and what was pouring down his face could have been tears, but most likely it was sweat.

Look, have some more of these, Father Sverko said and again put his hand in the pocket of his cassock.

And when he pulled his right hand out of the pocket

for a second time it was still full of dark red or almost black cherries with their stems in place, just as before; his pocket must have packed with fruit from the garden, and once more Signor Antonio bowed to Father Sverko and carefully picked some for himself, this time a cluster of three cherries.

The figs too are plentiful this year, the priest said while munching his cherries, though my husband had already claimed them as cherries from the garden and therefore belonging to the house, *our* house, last year I picked five baskets full of figs here in this garden, Father Sverko said, and this year it looks as if the crop will be even better.

Tell the priest that this house belongs to me, my sweetiepie whispered to me, although it wasn't quite true and besides he could have said so himself, as Father Sverko was speaking Italian only to be polite to Signora Nina and Signor Antonio, or maybe out of respect for the house.

But my husband's self-control was already slipping, I noticed that the priest was getting on his nerves just like Dimitrij and most of the other villagers get on his nerves, though right from the beginning I'd felt certain that it would have been better if he had stayed content with my little house and realized that the big one would be no good for us, and now he hadn't even thought to please me by greeting the priest.

Tell the priest that the house is mine, my husband whispered again, and I translated what he'd said, but made it sound less brusque, and for the first time Father Sverko turned to my husband and looked at him over the rim of his glasses.

So you've bought the house, he said, observing my sweetiepie with interest.

For one hundred million lire, Signora Nina said. That's the price we've agreed.

We haven't actually made up our minds yet, I said. But my husband is interested.

Father Sverko looked as if he were pondering what he'd just learnt and glanced around the room where we were standing, actually more like a closet than a real room. He also looked at the wall in front of us, from top to bottom, but as if he knew it well since long ago and as if the only reason for examining it so closely now was to convince himself that the wall still stood. He observed it for a long time and then he turned to my husband.

Well now, so you've bought the house, he said, not sounding at all surprised, using the same tone of voice as when he reads at Easter from the Gospels about Jesus nailed to the cross, asking his Father in Heaven to forgive mankind since one cannot demand much sense from people, and least of all any understanding of what they themselves are messing up.

For one hundred million lire, Signora Nina said, that's one hundred, Signor Antonio chimed in, and his voice was so weak that it didn't fit such a large sum; maybe it could have supported a smaller one, but not one hundred million lire.

The hundred million seemed too much for Signor Antonio's strength and in the darkness we could hear him fighting for air, his white nylon shirt was soaked with sweat and transparent despite the cool evening breeze now coming in through the open door and starting to sweep through the house. His shirt was sticking clammily to his chest and back, like the hen's down smeared on the bumper of the Baraldis' car on the other side of the wall, a shirt that once had been white and elegant, but no longer hid Signor Antonio's pale, obese body.

Father Sverko had turned from my husband to Signor Antonio, looking at him compassionately, even kindly. The dusk was settling over the garden outside the house and the priest had stopped chewing his cherries. His eyes rested on Signor Antonio and his face was as quiet and solemn as when he says Mass for us in Pelegrin and has just drunk the wine and wiped the Communion chalice dry. Again the room was silent and I wondered how all this would end, but there was still no end in sight, at least none I could imagine, even though the whole thing had been going on for more than long enough, and my only wish in this world was to get home and not have to translate any more, not one single word more.

A house must be cared for, Father Sverko said, and it seemed to me as if he were talking to all of us while looking at the wall my sweetie insisted on demolishing.

Surely you'll recall that the Holy Scripture tells us to see to our house before it is too late, the priest said, and

Signor Antonio tried to say something about roof tiles while Signora Nina looked at her watch, her gold watch glinting under her black net glove, but those who have faith need not fear, Father Sverko went on. Our Father will hold His hand over him and his house, over his exit as well as his entrance, and Signor Antonio said *Monsignore*, forgive me, but this house has but one door, the one we all came through, and Signor Antonio's breathing was coming in bursts, it was obvious that he'd found it hard to utter what he wanted to say, even though that wasn't much.

His strength seemed to be melting away, leaving him too weak to speak. Signora Nina's husband was fighting for air, which made his last words—"the one we all came through"—only pass his lips after great effort and then get sucked back inside him again with his next spasmodic intake of breath almost as soon as they'd emerged; and still he was right, you had to enter and leave this house by the very same door, though perhaps I was the only one who had understood what he had said, standing close enough to hear what to the others may have sounded more like panting, and while he had been struggling to say what he had on his mind Father Sverko had taken off his spectacles and polished them on his cassock, then put them back on his nose and looked benignly through them at Signor Antonio saying just so, my dear friend, exactly as Scripture tells us; and Signora Nina must have felt satisfied by what the priest had said about how Our Father holds His hand over both people and their houses, or at least over the people who have faith in Him, for now Signora Nina was through with the house.

Now you've seen all you need to see, she said and Father Sverko clasped his hands together and looked as if he was of the same opinion, in spite of having no special reason for being concerned about the empty house at all.

Let's go and see how my toad's doing, he said suddenly. There's a toad in the garden, it lives in the well.

A real toad, Signor Antonio panted, is it true?

Yes, indeed, a nice little fellow, the priest said and walked out of the room ahead of us, leading the way through the hall where the door had been left open, the four of us following him out of the house, out of *our* house, just as we had followed Signora Nina into it, and when we had walked round to the back of the house and were leaning over the edge of the well, looking into it, there really was a toad, quite still with only the top of his head and his eyes showing above the surface of the water, and Signora Nina shone her flashlight on it, but the toad didn't move.

Maybe it's already dead, Signor Antonio whispered.

Not at all, Father Sverko said, who had removed his spectacles again, and bending over more deeply than the rest of us into the mouth of the well, he started imitating a toad, croak, croak the echo answered from inside the well, but the toad made no sound, it neither responded nor even moved, and Signor Antonio too was leaning forward over the edge of the well, almost as far as the priest, when his wife suddenly took one step back, Toni, Signora Nina said sternly and then turned to the priest, my husband is very ill and easily gets dizzy, she explained and went on to tell Father Sverko what we already knew, that her husband during their visit to Pisa had refused to leave the city without first getting up to the top of the leaning tower, because of the view, she added, but on the way up he had been overwhelmed by vertigo and almost fainted, it was the heat, Signor Antonio said, my husband fainted halfway to the top, we had to phone for an ambulance, his wife told the priest, I did get to the top of the tower, her husband said, no, you didn't dare to, Signora Nina said, but her husband protested; I did, he said, not to the very top, his wife insisted, that you didn't dare, and Father Sverko had started polishing his glasses on his cassock again.

My husband could have died in Pisa, Signora Nina told the priest.

When I looked out I was on the wrong side of the tower, Signor Antonio said, nonsense, his wife said, I was looking straight into the sky, Signor Antonio said, and it was that view, all Heaven and no Earth, which had made him feel very insecure, you got dizzy, Signora Nina said, I no longer could see the ground below, her husband told us, that's exactly what I've been saying, Signora Nina said, but her husband, now with firm ground under his feet here in the garden and no longer high above it in a leaning tower, had once again bent far forward over the edge of the well and was looking down into it; in this garden of the house that he had never felt at home in, his wife had no power over him, but at the bottom of the well the toad stayed as immobile as ever.

It doesn't want to get up, Signor Antonio said, sounding disappointed.

Fa freddo, Signora Nina said and shivered. She had clasped her hands round her shoulders as if wishing for a shawl to cover her thin summer blouse, but she must have meant the wind, for after such a hot day the garden was still not chilly at all.

But there actually was a cool evening breeze by now, a breeze that had begun to blow up towards us from the valley and over the top of the wall into the garden, my husband catches cold so easily, Signora Nina said, and the wind in the garden seemed to grow stronger, making the fragile branches and leafy canopies above us in the trees sway from side to side, and now Father Sverko seemed resigned to the absence of any answer coming for him out of the well, not the slightest sign of life in fact.

It doesn't want to get up, Signor Antonio said, still leaning into the well, although not as far down as the priest had been, and when Signor Antonio straightened up and looked doubtfully at Father Sverko, his ill-looking face glowed an oily white in the dusk.

My dear Signor Baraldi, Father Sverko said, of course it doesn't want to get up. After all, a toad is not human. It doesn't get weary of being what it is, it's not aspiring to be anything else than that.

Well now, imagine, Signor Antonio sighed.

He knows his place and stays there, Father Sverko said. A toad is content with his fate.

Such a sensible little fellow, Signor Antonio said, peering into the well again, and as the dark deepened around us in the garden, Father Sverko begun instructing him about the differences between animals and human beings, pointing out that unlike animals, human beings can be tormented by doubts so that a person can be uncertain about the rightness of his place in this world and finally come to ask himself if his life isn't wasted, indeed if he hasn't failed to grasp God's plan, and when I say *finally*, Father Sverko said to Signor Antonio, I am of course alluding to our earthly point of view, so different from the perspective of Our Lord, how did it get down there, Signor Antonio asked, but by now Father Sverko was concerned with heavenly matters and no longer with the toad in the well.

Our Lord foresees our end long before we can even guess at it ourselves, the priest told us in the darkening evening, but when we human beings say *finally*, it never seems too late for us as long as we're still here on earth. After all we're still existing at that stage and there's surely time enough to start all over again, or so we imagine, the priest said. But no, my dear Signor Baraldi! Our Lord knows more than we ordinary mortals can about both our lives and the time He has allotted to us, Father Sverko said, so when we finally ask ourselves if we're not throwing our lives away, still believing we might do something about it, like what, Signor Antonio asked, but Father Sverko didn't allow his train of thought to be interrupted, at the very moment when we perhaps feel that it's not too late yet to pull ourselves together and start all over again from the beginning and turn to Him, pleading with Him to let us carry out His plan for our lives, the priest said to Signor Antonio, then our time and strength only suffice to allow us to ask that one single question: have I thrown away my life?

Finally, that'll be all we've got the time and strength for, Father Sverko said, just this one question. Have I thrown away my life? But not time to do anything about it.

Can God really be so cruel, Signor Antonio asked.

Not cruel, Father Sverko answered him, not cruel at all. But only such trials can bring forward our true spirit, Father Sverko said, although I thought that the priest should have understood how tactless it was to talk of trials to someone as seriously ill as Signora Nina's husband, and Signor Antonio was staring past him into the darkness as if no longer listening and not wanting to listen, for it is by undergoing trials that our beings are shaped, the priest said, and only when someone has fought adversity and won has he found the way home.

Did not Jesus take upon Himself such a trial for all our sakes? On the cross? And didn't He soon afterwards return home to His Father's house? Only reconciling oneself to one's fate fulfills the divine plan, Father Sverko said, imagine, Signor Antonio said in his faint voice, the Church knows so much.

That's how it is, my dear Signor Baraldi, Father Sverko said, that's exactly how it is, and the words of the priest must have impressed Signor Antonio whose eyes were open so wide that I could see their whites shining in the dark.

Maybe the toad has it better, Signor Antonio whispered, and in the twilight that was quickly growing deeper around us I could no longer see his face as well as before, but I heard his teeth chattering, and then suddenly a strong gust of wind swept through the garden and the leafy canopies above our heads, and when Signor Antonio looked up towards the sky I could see the cold sweat gleam on his face, a cold sweat coming from deep inside, having nothing to do with the weather.

There's rain in the air, Father Sverko said.

Wind-torn clouds were chasing each other across the sky, showing between them sudden ragged gaps of pale gray, a last reminder of the day that had passed. The wind that had begun as an evening breeze was now growing in strength and the change in the weather was surprising us all, Signora Nina looked at her watch again and said Toni, it's far too late, we must be getting back, and as a goodbye reached out her hand to me and I held it, a hand that under the net glove felt gnarled and hard.

Also Father Sverko agreed that it was time to go home, high time, he said, although if we had been prepared to be patient for half an hour or so we would hear his toad croak, a croaking toad of course heralds rain, the priest said, but still, there's a time and a place for everything, and on that score there's no difference between animals and human beings, so we'd better accept that yet another of our days is coming to its end, Father Sverko said, indeed towards its fulfillment in the name of God, and to all this Signor Antonio was nodding; there was clearly nothing the priest had said that he felt like objecting to and instead he kept nodding in agreement, but seemingly without any real conviction, as if he hadn't really been listening properly to the priest, but still was down at the bottom of the well with the toad, in the world of animals, less dangerous after all than that of human beings.

So now we have watched the passing of yet another day, Father Sverko said and shook hands with both me and my sweetiepie, the priest's hand being soft and flabby, and while we were walking through the garden towards the gate in the wall, he reminisced about old days in this house and this garden, days spent in the company of Signora and Signor Baraldi when they still came up here to stay for a few weeks every summer, those long-gone happy days, true gifts from Our Lord, as Father Sverko called them; and I got the impression that the priest immediately regretted saying all this, that by recalling those happy days of the past he rather unhappily managed to remind Signor Antonio of his illness, but that it all was too late now.

He had already made his mistake; now the past happy days were there with us, joining all the unhappy ones that had followed, and the priest had no choice but trying to

RICHARD SWARTZ

cover up his tactlessness by continuing to talk about the happiness of those past times as if they had been quite unremarkable, nothing special, as if the chain of happy days in our lives is endless, lasting forever and unaffected by any illness in the world, all this in order to show that it couldn't have been Signor Antonio's serious condition that he'd had in mind when he so carelessly associated just the past with happy days in the house and its garden, and to rid them of both illness and unhappiness once and for all, he recalled an absent friend, of course those were the days when your friend from Trieste came to stay here quite often, Father Sverko said to Signora Nina and Signor Antonio.

Remember? That friend of yours from Trieste who was with us so often, relaxing here in the garden and enjoying the view, the priest went on, your friend who liked to wear a white suit in the summer and used to say that he felt so much more comfortable with you here in your house and garden than in his own home in Trieste, Father Sverko said. Remember? Such an amiable and quiet person, Father Sverko said and Signora Nina agreed with him at once, it was always his opinion that we should sell the house, Signora Nina added, we were hardly ever here, her husband said, but Father Sverko asked for the name of their friend; I have forgotten the name of your friend, he said, and Signor Antonio mentioned the name, or rather breathed it out in an exhalation, unable to do more than pant his friend's name, so that I would never have figured out whom the priest was talking about, had I not guessed that it was Luigi Tartini, Signor Antonio's friend and colleague from the Trieste Post Office.

I'm sorry, what was that, Father Sverko said to Signor Antonio, Signor Tartini, Signora Nina answered and looked at her watch again, that's it, the priest exclaimed, that's the name I'm after, Tartini, Tartini, that's the friend who visited you so often.

But then, it was such a long time ago, the priest said. How time flies! Though I'm certain I saw him the other day down in Buzet, Father Sverko said, and Signora Nina and Signor Antonio both looked as if they thought they must have misheard him, as if Signor Antonio's friend had been absent from their lives for so many years that the priest could only have been talking about somebody else.

Impossibile, Signora Nina said and I could see that she truly felt the cold now, I certainly did, the priest said, it was your friend Tartini all right, it can't be true, Signor Antonio said, and you could see that what Father Sverko was saying about his old friend had touched him much more than the priest's discourse on trials and the house in heaven which had given Signor Antonio no comfort at all and hadn't interested my sweetiepie either, not anywhere near as much as his empty house of stone that was not yet his; and in the dark we all walked together through the garden towards the gate in the wall and there we said farewell. If I were in your shoes I'd stay here for a bit and get acquainted with the property I'd just bought,

Signora Nina said to us, but she had already locked the house and must have put the keys in her handbag, Beppo will lock up once you've left, she said and smiled; it was the first time I'd seen Signora Nina smile, a quick, almost shy smile, *addio*, my husband said, at least that much Italian he knows and must have felt particularly keen to demonstrate it now, in his own garden, and then we closed the gate in the wall and listened to them wandering down the gravel path on the other side

It's all over now, I said to my sweetie when we were alone in the garden on our side of the wall, in the garden of *our* house.

Everything is over now, I said and took his hand in mine, but just as I said that we heard steps on the gravel path on the other side again, the gate hinges squeaked and in the dusk a figure hurried through the garden towards us, but the dark sky and the shadows of the trees swallowed him, and it was only when he came close to us did I realize who it was.

It was Signor Antonio.

Scusateci, he panted once he had tottered up the path close enough to where we were standing in front of the house, excuse us, and then he ejected one by one the words following his excuse, and in spite of the deepening twilight I could see that sweat driven by the chill inside him once again covered his forehead, please, you must excuse us, Signor Antonio panted, breathing in with a gurgling sound, but we've never done this before, neither bought nor sold anything.

For a short while he stood silently in front of us with his head lowered and we could hear how he was fighting for breath, for more air.

Siamo persone molto semplici, Signor Anonio said, still looking down and we said nothing, neither my sweetie nor I, and nothing did I translate, nor did my husband ask me to.

Yes, Signor Antonio went on, repeating what he had just said, but now as if talking to himself, very simple people, and still Signor Antonio hadn't lifted his eyes from the ground and so we were kept standing there, all three of us feeling ashamed even though we could hardly see each other in the dark.

No one said anything, not my sweetiepie either, and then suddenly from the other side of the wall we heard Signora Nina's voice, Toni, she was calling, where are you, we must leave now, and Signor Antonio started just as he had once back in his home in Trieste when his wife accused him of never being able to complete anything properly, and Signora Nina's husband raised his head, looked at my sweetie and me and whispered *scusateci*.

Once more he asked us to forgive him, but now the Italian word meant something different than before, and as suddenly as he had appeared he now turned on his heel and stumped down the path towards the gate, back to his car and his wife waiting for him on the other side of the wall, and on the way he called out to her, so loudly I could not understand where the voice came from so suddenly, *vengo, vengo,* Signor Antonio shouted, I'm coming, I'm coming, and I hadn't imagined Signor Antonio being able to run so quickly with those small steps of his; and he was gone.

Soon we heard a car door slam and then a car start and drive off, but first a laugh came from the other side of the wall, sudden laughter in the dark. And Signora Nina was laughing more shrilly and for longer than the priest did, only Signor Antonio wasn't laughing at all or, at least, we couldn't hear him.

It's all over now, I whispered into my sweetie's ear.

He had put his arm round my shoulders and I whispered to him again, can you hear what I say, I whispered, it's all over now, and he whispered the same words back to me, over now, he whispered into my ear, what do you mean by that, and this was the moment when I realized that nothing was over, that perhaps nothing had even quite started yet, and against my will I had to look once more towards the night sky; towards the sky without stars above our heads, and there was nothing there to be seen, not even a moon in the darkness.